# THE DENIALIST'S ALMANAC OF AMERICAN PLAGUE AND PESTILENCE

# The Denialist's Almanac of American Plague and Pestilence

## Christopher Mohar

This publication is made possible by the funding provided by the Shaheen College of Arts and Sciences and the English Department at the University of Indianapolis. Special thanks to IngramSpark and to those students who judged, edited, designed, and published this chapbook: Jeffery Dixon, Mercadees Hempel, Spencer Martin, and James Nelligan.

UNIVERSITY *of*
**INDIANAPOLIS**®

Published by

Etchings Press
1400 E Hanna Avenue
Indianapolis, IN 46227
All rights reserved.

blogs.uindy.edu/etchings/
www.uindy.edu/cas/english

Printed by IngramSpark
ingramspark.com

Published in the United States of America

ISBN 13: 978-0-9988976-7-7

23 22 21 20 19 18 17    2 3 4 5
Second Printing, 2019

*For Madge*

Faustus: Stay, Mephistopheles, and tell me, what good will
my soul do thy lord?
Mephistopheles: Enlarge his kingdom.
Faustus: Is that the reason he tempts us thus?
Mephistopheles: *Solamen miseris socios habuisse doloris.*
—Christopher Marlowe
*The Tragicall History of the Life and Death of Doctor Faustus*

# 1

## T. Wodehouse Brinkley

The torrential rain of frogs falling in his lawn was not the first thing T. Wodehouse Brinkley noticed when he removed his Eyebeam goggles and exited his nine-hour marathon gaming session of *Nether Realms II*, nor did Wode notice the blood-colored cloud diffusing through the upper limits of the sky like the after-gasp of a snuffed-out, mountain-sized cigarette butt. For whatever reason—perhaps the precise focal distance to which his eyes had acclimatized during his extended immersion in the virtual world, or his yen for climbing a particular yew tree in the front yard (Wode's only habitual form of exercise)—the first thing Wode noticed was that single flickering yew. The tree flittered like a faulty pixel, there one nanosecond, gone the next. Visible, invisible. Tangible, intangible. Wode looked at it, looked through it, and blinked. To the extent that he registered it at all, he figured it for an illusion caused by his re-emergence, a neurological form of *the bends* experienced upon surfacing too quickly into reality. Because the Eyebeam so thoroughly altered human consciousness, it was not unusual for the nervous system to require a readjustment interim, but this was the first time Wode had ever experienced a full-on hallucination.[1]

"Suck it," Wode said to no one in particular. The Eyebeam's sweat-damp membrane released itself from his forehead with a burp as he pulled back the device and wore it atop his hairline, as a surfer might a pair of Ray-Bans. His eyes felt scorched and peeled. His BO was a sickening-yet-pleasing mingle of bellybutton, deodorant, cumin, and ass. His underwear's elastic chafed his bacne. His quest for Bandorff the Elder's elixir had just ended catastrophically and he was none too happy to have returned to Earth. And who could blame him? Earth sucked. Consider Wode's typical daily routine: hide from Brian Peters behind cafeteria dumpsters while other students mingle; listen to raccoons gorge themselves on rancid French toast sticks in said dumpster; fall asleep and/or get diarrhea in homeroom; Health; Home Ec; Algebra; surrender Nutty Bar and PB&J

---

1 Documented side effects of long-term Eyebeam immersion include: nausea, headache, dizziness, blurred vision, irritability, excessive sweating, hypertension, loss of sensation in the tongue, visual and auditory hallucinations, constipation, diarrhea, pink eye, decreased libido, phototoxicity, restless leg syndrome, tinnitus, xeroderma, paresthesia, amnemonic aphasia, akathisia, and bruxism.*

*(Not insignificantly, these side effects were more or less the same as those on the warning label of Funcshunil™, a popular neoteric pharmaceutical prescribed to combat the symptoms of videogame-induced "bends.")

to Brian Peters; watch Brian Peters eat Nutty Bar and throw PB&J into urinal; Gym (which induced nerd v. jock sufferings so stereotypical as to warrant no further comment and to almost be laughable, if they weren't so utterly painful); Biology; the hour of detention served daily in place of his former spot in Advanced Computer Programming III, which had been the only class Wode enjoyed, the solace he'd looked forward to every day until he was banned from school computers for life for hacking into the administrative network and changing Brian Peters' grades and editing the "Comments" section of each course record, e.g.: *Brian Peters is an above-average DICKHOLE and real TURDBURGLAR to have in the classroom.* Pretty much everyone—including some teachers—referred to Wode as "Toad" or "Toadhouse" to his face, not to mention who-knows-what-else they called him behind his back, and when he got home from school, his mother presented him every afternoon with the exact same list of chores: *Clean Litter Box, Put Away Dishes, Do Some Pushups and Sit-ups, Wash Your Face, Pray 12 Rosaries.* So what motive could Wode have to spend any time in the "real" world, where he was simultaneously hungry and diarrheal, where his actions had no meaning, could change nothing, where his own mother insinuated that he was repugnant? Why would he want to be Toad when he could be Lothar The Destroyer, savior of the entire Kingdom of Nether, who could decapitate orcs with a single cleave of his battle-axe, who possessed arcane spells of teleportation and telekinesis, who currently had a Melee Combat Rating of

641 and a nigh-invulnerable Defense Rating of 844? Wode knew the Eyebeam's fantasies were trivial and escapist. He simply didn't care. But, like a dolphin or sea turtle, he had to come up to breathe eventually, so here he was trying to wipe the implausible vision from his eyes, while the yew tree continued to dis- and re-appear.

The yew was a wind-beaten beast of a tree, all knuckled-up and gnarled like an artless bonsai cooked large by a growth-ray. Its serpentine trunk and drooping fronds could've slipped straight from the pages of a *Weird Fantasy* comic, and for that reason it was the single feature of extant reality that Wode approved of in the domestic landscape that his parents had otherwise groomed towards the preternatural boringness shared ubiquitously throughout the cookie-cutter subdivision of Highland Heights, in Balta, Wisconsin: ChemTru lawn, flagstone walk, crawling junipers mulched in pea-gravel.

The tree's visual jitter was reminiscent of the occasional instance in *Nether Realms II* wherein a persistent bug in the code would cause a labyrinth wall to go blinking in and out of transparency. If your avatar stepped beyond the event horizon of the glitch, he would get sucked inside and caught forever between the worlds of the permeable and the impenetrable: both within the wall and without, forever jiggered into that liminal space from which there was no escape—you were frozen solid as Han Solo in carbonite or a flea in fossilized amber. Sure, a battle-axe-wielding, chainmail-hauberk-wearing flea, no doubt, but a flea nonetheless. The only thing to do was a manual reboot, which was no good for the hardware, and, worse yet, if you pulled the plug without logging off of your account, any progress that your character had made through the dungeon would not be saved beyond the last checkpoint. This was precisely what had just happened to Wode to ruin his aeonian gaming session, and he'd therefore lost two dozen enchanted gems from his inventory, which, to think about it made him physically ill.

Wode's bodily needs felt sudden but in actuality had ebbed on through an erosive process of persistent neglect. He wobbled to his feet, slugged the dregs of a tepid MTN Dew, and slunk to the bathroom. The life processes that happened therein need not be further described, save to say that they were long overdue and that symptoms of mild dehydration were apparent.

As Wode returned to his bedroom, the sound of his parents' angry voices rose from the direction of the kitchen, though too quietly for Wode to make out what they were fighting about. He closed his door with the intention of resting his eyes for a moment and then returning to his game. But before he could again don the Eyebeam goggles, the colossal croaking noise reverberating through the walls called his attention to the conditions outside and the blur of falling frogs caught his eye. Throngs of fallen frogs lay in various states of injury—from exploded, dead-limbed, and disemboweled to miraculously intact and hoppy, roiling happily throughout the ChemTru lawn and spewing about in the street. The downpour slowed, but a light drizzle of amphibians continued—the occasional green blur with flailing, rubbery limbs whizzed by the window. The ribbiting and croaking was unfathomable. Wode noticed, too, the bloody thunderhead devouring the sky and the yew tree still flickering like a fluorescent bulb trying and failing to fire in a dark room. Then it blinked hard, and was gone.

Wode gasped. The foot of panic kicked awake a nervous hornet's nest in his guts. Was he brain-scrambled by video games? Insane? Was this a "schizophrenic break?" Had he confused the real and the virtual worlds such that his actual identity was Lothar the Destroyer? Perhaps "Wode" was the fiction. Perhaps the truth lay in Lothar's crusade for the Draconian Elixir that would restore the fallow Kingdom of Nether to health—a magic potion powerful enough to heal the parched-mud earth and invigorate its desiccated wheat fields until they literally wept, watercolor-like, their excesses of emerald-green. Perhaps this was the life-or-death quagmire upon which the fate of the known world rested, and that other so-called life, that doldrum of farts and algebra homework and breakfast cereal, might be nothing more than a mystical simulacrum, a dream evoked in the subconscious mind while the warrior's body made camp for the night by bedroll and torchlight, hoping to recover a few Life Points and Magic Points in communion, not with semiconductors and electrons, but with sorcery and Gnostic truth, maybe?

Nope. This bullshit life was real. As was whatever-it-was

happening outside his window. Had Wode not recently voided himself, the bodily tremor of this recognition might have been disastrous.[2]

Wode ran for his parents. His sock-feet slid when he hit the hardwood, and he glided to a stop just behind the kitchen island. His mother and father hadn't seen him. Together they gazed out the sliding-glass doors. The back lawn was just as frog-chocked as the front had been.

"Have you—" Wode began, but swallowed it. Something was wrong. His mother was weeping. His father hugged her but she slapped his arm away. Wode almost couldn't bear to watch, so pulled the Eyebeam goggles down over his eyes, a comfort reflex like sucking his thumb. Hidden there in the darkness of the powered-off goggles, he listened.

"You can't argue with God," his mother said. "You can't tell him which rules you'd like bent on your behalf."

"Jesus, Eileen, we're a married couple."

"Jesus Christ is Lord, not a curse word. What don't you understand about *forever*?"

"All that stuff about pillars of salt—that's for the homos. All that immolation by brimstone. Sodomites. It's different when you're married."

"And yet."

"There has to be an explanation."

"There is: it's *your* fault, you, you... scoundrel! You

---

2 Although, really, what constitutes "disastrous" during an apocalypse?

tricked me. Ordered wine with dinner to impair my judgment. And now *look*!"

Wode took his mother's words too literally, but when he peeled back the goggles to see what she was looking at, nothing had changed. Nothing except that a rogue frog had worked its way up the back porch stairs, then attempted—thumped—and failed to jump through the window glass. Wode's father glanced at the pitiful creature. He brushed a fallen strand of hair from his wife's eyes.

"Why would God give us these bodies if he didn't want us to—"

"Mom? Dad? Something's wrong." Wode stepped wobbly from his hiding spot. Eileen's eyes were bloodshot from crying and her flower-print cardigan hung off by one buttonhole. Randy's oxford was rolled at the wrist to reveal a heavy gold watch. Sweat stains bloomed from his armpits. His pupils flitted behind square-rimmed glasses like panicked rodents in live-trap cages. "I'm freaked," Wode said. "What's happening?"

"It's probably nothing," his father said. "A freak weather event. These phenomena occur under improbable but not impossible meteorological conditions, then they blow over."

"For goodness sake, Randy! You can't always shelter the boy." Wode's mother took his face tight in both hands. "It's the Rapture, Wode. And we're not going."

"The Rapture?"

"They're all gone. Everyone I've tried to call. Marybeth, Judy Jo, Pastor John and his whole family. Gone. Oh, God, help us we're still here—" Quivering, she wrapped Wode in her flabby arms and itchy acrylic. "Oh, Torchester, my baby, I wanted so much more for you."[3]

Mom's hug smooshed the Eyebeam goggles atop his hair into a precarious position, and Wode stretched one hand up to keep them from falling, the other still hugging his mother. Upon feeling this fidgeting, Eileen released her hug and reached for Wode's Eyebeam. "Take this off, honey."

"No, Mom! Leave it. I'm not even playing. I just want to wear it."

"These may be your last moments on Earth and you want to spend them—"

------

3 Wode hated the name Torchester, which made even less sense than Wodehouse, which didn't make all that much sense to begin with, given that his parents names were Randall Richard Brinkley and Eileen Gael Brinkley nee Doyle, so why would they have a son and name him Torchester Wodehouse? Wode guessed they maybe thought it sounded sophisticated or something. But really all it meant was that he was "Toad." Online, he went by the handle "Torch" which he felt made him sound badass, if only in a nondescript-vanilla-badass sort of way. But in real life, Torch was still a pimpled, four-foot-two, mildly overweight thirteen-year-old with the unfortunate habit of wearing thrift-store Army t-shirts in the hopes that this, too, would make him seem tougher—shirts with pictures of skulls bearing green berets and seraphic wings, with bayonets crossed before a rearguard of flames and slogans like "Kill 'em all and let God sort 'em out" or "Mercenaries never die, they just go to hell to regroup." This tactic worked about as well as you might guess it would.

"Let's nobody argue at a time like this," Randy said. He stood over them, his arms a desperate net trying to bind the family together. "Who knows, Eileen? Maybe the process happens in waves. Maybe there's still time to repent and renew your vows, say a prayer—"

"My mother! Oh goodness, we have to check on Mom!" Eileen leapt to her feet. Randy already had his cell phone. On screen, the words *Gma Doyle @ Mother of Mercy Hosp* were trailed by the faint pulse of animated ellipses.

  .

  . . .

  . . . . . .

  .

  . . .

  . . . . . .

  .

  . . .

  . . . . .

"Line's dead," Randy said. Eileen wore the expression of a pole barn on the verge of collapse; the slightest breeze could've crumpled her in on herself. Randy again took her in his arms, and this time she allowed him to.

"You stay here and pray. Ask for forgiveness for all of us. Wode and I will go look for your Mom."

"I don't want to be left alone."

"Then pray in the car. Let's go."

"First let me grab my rosary."

When Eileen was out of earshot, Randy whispered to

Wode through clenched teeth. "Bitch better not be raptured. Jesus Christ, if that old crone got beamed up and I didn't, I swear to God…"

Wode was afraid, but part of him was also screaming with desire, telling him, *this is it, this is it, this is it,* though he wasn't precisely sure what it was—the implosion of his life that he had somehow always hoped for? A chance to be a hero? A chance to experience something greater than being a weak, overweight kid immersed in his videogames alone in his room? Something was different. Something was happening.

Eileen returned, and, in the first unified family activity the three of them had undertaken in untold weeks, the Brinkleys piled into the Land Rover.

# 2

# LYLE DENIAL

Lyle awakened to a thrumming hydrostatic pressure on his braincase. He was pleased to find himself still pleasantly stoned, however, rather than being stoned and drunk, he was now stoned and hungover: the world droned like a shitty sludge-metal band at a basement show, like a bad comedown from too much ecstasy, like a pantheon of morlocks chanting a malevolent dirge from the bowels of the city sewers. This headache, man. For realzies. And what the Christ was that thumping? A hailstorm?

On the graffiti-tagged coffee table rested a pizza box opened flat as a book with a broken spine, from which Lyle extricated the final room-temperature slice before kicking the box to the carpet to make room for his crossed feet. The mouthful of plasticized cheese helped cleanse the taste of whiskey/bile/gingivitis. Passed-the-hell-out in ostrich-skin boots, that was a first. But only because of the boots, which were pawn-shop-new as of yesterday. And yeah, whatever, he was in hella debt, but for thirty-five bucks?

Somewhere below him, something vibrated and emitted an agitated chirp. He fished blind below the couch cushions until he caught his cell phone. His email was angry with him.

But that thumping. Jesus. That hailstorm must be a bad one. But because of all the boarded-over windows elsewhere, nowhere in the living room offered a vantage to the outdoors. Lyle chomped the 'za as he headed to the bathroom, kicking aside whatever junk lay in his path: unopened mail, empty prescription drug blister-packs, a bicycle wheel, a cabasa that shuddered its rattlesnake shudder as it fled for the darkness below the TV console. Like so many young men of his generation, Lyle had expertly honed his ability to self-induce a state of hypnotic tunnel vision while engaging with any LED-backlit device, and thus—although he stood near enough the window to feel the sunlight glaze a swath across the hollow of his neck and to sense the croaking sound not as merely an aural wallpaper but as a physical oscillation of air pressure reverberating the very walls of the house— Lyle did not devote a mere half-second to glance out the window, but lingered beside it thumbing his device, poised to take said glance out said window at his next earliest convenience. He crammed the final cheesy bite into his maw, tossed the crust in the general direction of the trash, unslung his junk from his jeans, and proceeded to piss and continue to dick with his phone.

Email: two spams, a message from Billie[1] that he deleted without reading, then undeleted, the deleted again, and a fourth piece of mail from a sender named **PRPC AUTONOTIFY**, which Lyle was prepared to delete, too, but something in the subject line rang a familiar chord through the ganja-patinated brass of his mental wind chimes.

> *To: "Lyle Denial" <LyreLyre@MailMail.com>*
> *From: "PRPC AUTONOTIFY" <AUTONOTIFY@PostRapturePetCare.Net>*
> *Date: September 3, 2012*
> *Subj: URGENT. You've been ACTIVATED. MEMBER#2797*
>
> *Dear Non-Christian Pet Lover:*
> *If you're receiving this missive, the End of Days is upon us. The faithful among us who know Jesus Christ as our lord and savior are arisen, and the time has come for you to fulfill your duty as a Post-Rapture Pet Care Technician. While we recognize that you surely face the terror of a tumultuous fallen world and the shocking recognition of the falsity of your professed non-Christian*

---

1 Lyle's on-again, off-again girlfriend—mostly off, lately—to whom he owed $350 that he'd borrowed two weeks ago when he couldn't make rent. Instead of putting the cash to its intended use, though, Lyle had obtained a vast quantity of psychotropic substances, gotten evicted, had the Telecaster he'd forgotten in the apartment unrepentantly repossessed by his former landlord as collateral, and moved in with his bass player, Trevor, which is more or less how he ended up awakening hung-over on Trevor's sofa this very morning.

spiritual beliefs, we urge you to remane[2] steadfast and stalwart in this moment of uncertainty and to uphold your duties to which you solmnly[3] vowed yourself upon registering with PostRapturePetCare. Net's surrogate caregiver program. Our faithful clients, who, like you, are pet lovers, look down from on high with gratitude. The care you bestow upon their beloved companions shall not go unappreciated. Below please find the description and whereabouts of the companions to which you have been assigned as guardian and caregiver:

Registration: 85xty6793n
Name: Muffin
Species: Purebred Siamese
Description: Purebred Siamese
Owner: Linda Berkshire
Location: 1622 Melody Lane, Balta, WI
Contact: (608)-555-3840, LindaBerk02@mWire.net

Registration: n9047nfrh7
Name: Ralph Waldo "Obama" DeVries
Species: dog/mutt
Description: M, white snout, black dapple coat, white boots, one blue eye, one brown, approx. 45 lbs. Likes bananas, cheese, ear scratching.
Owner: Phillip & Lew DeVries
Location: 19 Watershed St, Apt B, North Balta, WI
Contact: LewD@Mailmail.com, (608)-555-0192

Registration: 101m00setk

---

2 [sic]
3 [sic]

*Name: Ladybird*
*Species: miniature dachshund*
*Description: F, wire-haired, piebald black and tan*
*Owner: Moira Doyle*
*Location: Mother of Mercy Care Community, Room 113,*
*424 West Lakefront Drive, Balta, WI*
*Contact: (608)-555-3984, ext. 113*

*Upon successfully retrieving each of your charges out of harm's way and relocating them to a place of sanctuary, you may claim your $200 per pet "Care and Service" stipend. Simply use your existing user ID and password to logi n to our secure server: <https://www.PostRapturePetCare.net/financal/claims.aspx>*
*Please note that PostRapturePetCare.Net cannot be held liable in the event of a computer hardware or software failure resultant from worldly conditions of post-apocalyptic bedlam, including but not limited to: riots; national or international currency devaluation; electric, electronic, or fiber-optic infrastructure failure; floods, hail, brimstone, and other natural disasters; locusts; boils; plagues; and all other potentially detrimental conditions of a post-Rapture landscape, whether foreseeable or unforeseen, intentional or unintentional, natural or anthropogenic or divine. Failure to have pre-registered in PRPC's automated payment system with direct-deposit banking information may result in loss or delay of payment.*
*While our automated payment service works on the "honor system," and our founding members are necessarily absent from the corporeal earth and thus unable to "police" your fulfillment of your contractual obligations, we trust you to do the right thing. Should your payment fail to transfer, your moral compass (atheistic as it may well be) should nonetheless guide you to fulfill your obligations to the greatest extent possible.*

> A righteous man cares for the needs of his animal,
> but the kindest acts of the wicked are cruel.
> —*Proverbs 12:10*

*Please know that as we gaze down from the heavens, we will be praying for the best for you and new companions in this fallen world.*

*God bless,*
*Marybeth Bergmann and Siobhan Ward,*
*Founders, PostRapturePetCare.Net*

"Holy bat shit," Lyle said. He clicked the link to the secure server, logged in, and confirmed that, yes, he had indeed saved all three pets and should be awarded $600 by electronic deposit. "Easiest money I ever—JESUS!"

A frog smacked the window alongside his head, leaving a frogprint of blood on the glass. Lyle finally glanced up from his phone to notice the roiling multitudes of amphibians swarming over every visible surface—street, lawn, sidewalk, etcetera. The rain gutters of the neighbor's house spilled over with them, and the bed of Trevor's pickup truck was filled by layer upon layer of green bodies. Lyle leapt back from the window, slipped on a stray pizza crust, and smacked his forehead against the shower stall. Urine-dripping penis still limp in his hand, he crumpled to the insipid bathroom tile, and the world faded to black.

Lyle dreamed that a talking dog-woman nuzzled his

chest and nuzzled close to bark-whisper the lyrics of "Vi Har Aldri Levd," Lyle's favorite song by Dødsønske Drøm.[4]

*Plague of locust*
*scorch o'er the land.*
*We'll drink the blood*
*blood of the lamb.*

*Barn av tidens krefter*
*de hadde rett vi kom til helvete*
*Barn av tidens krefter*
*de hadde rett vi kom til helvete.*[5]

---

4 A Norwegian black-metal band notorious for being founding members of the New Aryan Church of Odin and for a series of highly-publicized, probable-but-unproven church burnings, as well as for their being the launching pad for the from-jail solo career of singer/songwriter Vargr Vindheim, who, having been convicted of stabbing his mailman with a pair of scissors, was sentenced to eight years in the Ullersmo Federal Penitentiary, where he was denied access to guitars, drums, and the like, but was able to obtain a cassette deck and small synthesizer, on which he recorded a series of manipulated tape loops and simulated orchestral funeral dirges, released later in a three-CD box-set entitled *Tarmarbeid* and accompanied by commemorative photos of Vargr Vindheim playing basketball in the prison gym, raking leaves in the prison lawn, fingering his keyboard in his prison cell, etcetera.

5 "The children of tomorrow's forces / They were right, we went to hell".

When Lyle awakened, his head killed. The frogs were still outside. The sky had further darkened to a deep sanguine hue, and the clouds had nucleated into a colossal slow-motion funnel cloud, a maelstrom the thickness of a chocolate malt and the color of a menstrual clot, from which lightning emitted at regular intervals. Lyle prepared a couple good bong rips to take the edge off of his harp-strung brain, double kick-drum pulse, and tremolo-twitching fingertips, not to mention the throbbing hangover headache he'd worsened by thwacking his braincase against the shower stall. Then he went upstairs and softly kicked awake Trevor where he slept on a bare futon pad.

"Go to hell." Trevor smacked his lips as if his mouth were full of mud.

"We might be right at this very minute actually doing exactly that and I am so not kidding it's not even funny except I don't believe in hell seeing as how I'm an atheist though I have to admit I'm starting to rethink now the whole atheism thing or at a bare minimum maybe I'm thinking like maybe agnostic at least for now while we see how this whole apocalypse thing pans out." Lyle set the smoldering drug paraphernalia on the floor near Trevor's face. "This first, then look outside."

After Trevor had executed his own requisite bong rips, pulled on his patch-covered black nuthuggers with the pyramid-spiked belt still through the loops, and gone downstairs to witness firsthand the mind-bending scene that precipitated outside his bathroom window, he and Lyle talked themselves from panicked to calm to panicked again, at which point Trevor remembered the Klonopin stashed in the come-down-kit he'd assembled during the brief period last fall in which he'd flirted with the idea of getting heavily into blow.

Lyle dampened a towel and scrubbed the buffered coating off of three Klonopin tablets. He used the butt of a screwdriver to pulverize the friable interiors to a fine powder on the clean underside of a filthy dinner plate.[6] After digging a piece of his sliced-in-half credit card out of the kitchen garbage, he cut some lines. The sedatives permeated the capillaries of Lyle's nasal passages, dissolved into his bloodstream and traveled brainward, toward the locus of isolated little folds of brain that, thanks to Catholic School, still feared the wrath of God—albeit in a sort of knee-jerk, guilt-driven manner—and was pretty busy contemplating the "What If's" of his current scenario.

"I hope this isn't the *end* end," Lyle said.

"What're you, afraid we got left behind?"

Yes.

"No. Are *you* scared?"

"No. Totally not."

"Me neither. Totally not scared. Not at all."

---

6 Thus bumping the instrument's current ratio of mortar-and-pestle-style-drug-preparation to actual screwdriving to around 7:3.

"Totally."

"More like I'm thinking: how can we go on tour next month if everyone is all raptured and there's no one to see the shows?"

"Like the same people who would get raptured even want to listen to us anyway," Trevor said.

"But if *it* is the *end* end—which I'm not necessarily saying it is, but hypothetically—what do you think is going to happen to us? I mean all this Satanic black metal and nihilism… what if our assumptions have been wrong all along?"

"Don't know. Didn't worry about it before I was born, don't think I'll worry about it after I'm dead."

"Do you think you've lived a good life?"

"Meh. I mean, what does that even mean?"

Lyle, for one, did not think he had. It's not like he didn't know he was a substance-abusing loser whose never-gonna-happen pipedreams of rockstardom were nothing but the shallow estuary of his defense mechanisms lapping ineffectually against the pelagic waters of his lacking self-esteem and his oceanic sense of life's purposelessness. It's not like he didn't know it was hard on Billie to come out to Club Pink or The Hell Hole after working a double shift at Mother of Mercy, plus to regularly pay his delinquent phone bills, drive him around, cook him dinner, be a constant emotional cheerleader in support of his heavy metal dreams, etcetera. Hell, that's why she'd dumped him, right? His narcissistic focus on his rock career was pretty much why every girlfriend ever had dumped him, ever. He was well enough aware of these flaws. It's just that he didn't often look at them head-on, didn't know what else to do about any of it except to, as Journey might say, "Don't Stop Believing." It was perhaps a stupid belief, but a genuine one, this hope that if he were on stage before a throng of cheering fans, his life wouldn't feel so empty any more—like maybe if all those people collectively loved him, he wouldn't have to do the hard work of figuring out how to love himself. Like maybe then he could stand to wake up in the morning and look in the mirror and be himself, and not have to crank up this mental fog-machine between his incarnation and his reflection to drown out that reality, with the aforementioned fog-machine consisting mainly of pot and pills but sometimes mushrooms, coke, E, whatever someone passed him at a party.

"I've got a mission," Lyle said, "that you should help me with." He explained to Trevor the errand of recovering the rapture-abandoned pets from his email list.

"We can take the bitchmobile," Lyle suggested.

"Empty."

"I'll fill it up. I already got paid for the doggie gig."

"Then why bother following through?"

Because I need to do at least one good thing before my time's up, Lyle did not say. "You're a heartless bastard, you know that?" He poked a finger into Trevor's sternum. "Think: you wake up one morning and you're totally without your people. Alone. How would you feel, man?

Huh? How would you feel?"

Trevor looked at his watch as if to double-check, re: the absence of scheduled conflicts in his slothful, unemployed, drug-addled schedule.

"None of this half-tank shit. I want it full," he said.

Lyle snowshoveled the frogs out of the bed of the truck while Trevor worked on the always-tenuous task of getting the engine to fire. Gas, bog, chugging ignition, repeat, etcetera. When they both succeeded, Trevor slid over to the passenger side and Lyle drove. Or, he would have driven, if not for the frogs.

"Do you remember Frogger?" Lyle asked. "For Atari? It's like Frogger out here, but backwards. Frogger gone terribly wrong."

"Just run them over," Trevor said.

"Dude, we are embarking on an animal-liberation mission. Do you not see the hella irony?"

"Well, I'm for one not going to sit in the driveway in the bitchmobile all day." Trevor made to leave the truck.

"Get back in." Lyle sifted through the thrift-store cassette tapes that littered the floor and seats and dash and cup-holders and map slots, giggling at the apropos irony as he flashed Trevor the cover of AC/DC's *Highway to Hell*, but ultimately he settled on Dio's *Lock Up the Wolves*. He cranked the stereo.

The heavy metal seemed to have the desired effect: frogs fled. Still, progress was erratic and slow at best, due to Lyle attempting to allow the frogs sufficient time to hop out of the way, which meant that the bitchmobile's MPH averaged out somewhere around a frog-hop pace. Unfortunately, the average frog-hop pace was slow enough to allow occasional fast-hopping frogs to spring from the sidewalks, outrun the truck, and plant themselves squarely in its path. One idiot bullfrog, a titan with yellow and black stripes around its eyes, refused entirely to leave the roadway and opted instead to hop in a straight line away from the oncoming pickup truck in a futile attempt to put distance between itself and the vehicle while remaining ceaselessly in its path. *How utterly like life*, Lyle thought. Trevor yelled, "Get out of the goddamn way, you narc!"

"Narc?" Lyle asked.

Trevor shrugged.

The Klonopin came on as a nice adjunct to the weed buzz, and Trevor felt a sense of peace and unity, like, *yeah the sky is all hurricaning blood and raining frogs and things are covered in bloodguts and very quiet, no traffic, empty cars stalled in the streets or some crashed out like people just disappeared while driving, but I don't mind that I'm still here, because this is my place in the world, it's happening this way because it has to happen this way, because this is how it's supposed to be, like, for us to be here while the world is tearing itself in half before our eyes and here we are mere humans, and rockstars or not, we're all gonna die so maybe, like, try to give something back first? We gotta save these dogs, man.*

"Yeah, that's what we're doing," Trevor said. "If you'd drive, anyway." Lyle hadn't realized he'd been speaking aloud. He had also, apparently, stopped the car. How long had he been staring at the sky?

He drove. To augment the heavy metal, Lyle also made a concerted effort toward frog clearing via honking, engine revving, leaning out the window to curse at top volume, and eventually he simply leveraged an increasing disregard for trampling the dying or already dead bodies as he became desensitized to the carnage.

"Just run them over," Trevor said. "They're a lesser species. And they're not exactly on the verge of going extinct. As you can see."

Something flickered in Lyle's peripheral. Something massive. But when he looked, there was nothing there. In fact, he could have sworn that the vacant area he was looking as had once been a split-level townhouse with its lower floor converted to a local deli. Maybe that was one block over, though?

"Didn't Radical Sandwich used to be there?" Lyle said. "Like, right *right* there?"

Trevor shrugged. But, no, Lyle was sure of it. It had been a favorite late-night spot of Billie's and she'd bought him a Reuben there many a time at 4 am after a gig. Now it wasn't even a vacant lot. More like negative space. A sort of white absence that seared Lyle's brain if he looked at it directly.

"Dude, how do you know these pets even need to be saved?" Trevor said. "What if this is not the Rapture but just some messed-up global warming hurricane?"

"In Wisconsin?"

"Well, did you try calling them? The people? Because

some of these holier-than-thou types go around secretly molesting little boys or buying prostitutes drugs and I bet a few of your clients are not even raptured. Not that I believe that's what's happening, the Rapture. Just saying."

"Good call. Ring them up." He tossed Trevor his cell phone and turned down the Dio.

"Yes, hi, I'm calling about Ralph Waldo Obama DeVries, please."

A man's voice answered with a string of profanity so loud that Trevor removed the phone to arm's length as if it were a sopping diaper. From across the car, Lyle could make out a few words, one of which seemed to be "cockbiter." Trevor tossed the phone on the dash.

"So we're not picking up Obama," he said.

Lyle guided the pickup into the neighborhood Gas Rite. An awning had kept the pavement relatively clear of frogs, and after all the crawling, that single second of smooth acceleration felt breakneck. At the pump, the credit card reader was down, so Lyle selected to Pay Inside.

"Who's next?" Trevor called out the window. "Muffin?"

"I'm allergic to cats. I specifically checked the 'no cats' box on my application."

"Sorry, Muffin. That leaves Ladybird."

Inside, no attendant presided over the store, and after several unsuccessful attempts to ring up his gas purchase on the register himself, Lyle decided to leave without paying. And while he was at it, hell, might as well snag a hotdog, right? The greasy tubes of meat rotated on glistening mechanized rollers below a sickly yellow heat lamp. But something was wrong with the dogs, something beyond just the requisite gas-station-level-grotesquerie. Lyle could see right through them. They were there and not there at once. Lyle wiped his eyes. The hotdogs flickered and disappeared. He was stoned, but he didn't think he was that stoned. He waited for the dogs to reappear, but they did not. Fine, he'd lost his appetite for them anyway. Lyle helped himself to a twelver of Sierra Nevada, a Pringles tube, and as many packages of beef jerky as he could carry, which he dumped into Trevor's lap when he returned to the pickup. Trevor cranked up the Dio even louder and raised his hand in the sign of the horns. Lyle gave him the horns back, and the two punched their fists together for a Lock and Shock, tremoring.

"Ladybird, here we come!" Trevor hollered through a mouthful of jerky.

Lyle thrust the pickup back into action at the fastest pace the frog-choked streets would allow.

# 3

## RALPH WALDO "OBAMA" DEVRIES



In the final hours before The Flood of Glory, Ralph Waldo "Obama" DeVries had not eaten for ten days and found himself sick with hunger to point of collapse. In his brickwork grotto behind a rusted dumpster, Obama managed to claw his sheet of corrugated cardboard out to a satisfactory flatness, but he had only the energy to complete two of his usual-requisite-three nose-to-hind circlings before he lay with his snout tucked below his tail and attempted sleep, though sleep would not come—for the earth was rumbling below him and thunder cracked overhead, and Obama's enervated hindquarters shook with fear, his tail tucked between his legs. Two more hours of thunder would rumble on before the rain of frogs began to fall, and in the meanwhile Obama was not yet aware that this storm was something other than a terrifying weather event. He knew only that there was no hamper to hide behind, no closet to cower in. He was alone.

It had not always been this way. Three weeks earlier, during those first golden days after the triumphant advent of his Third Bloodless Liberation, food had been plentiful, if intermittent, for Obama. Immediately upon effecting his escape through the picket bastions of his backyard prison, Obama had come upon the freshkilled corpse of an albino squirrel still twitching in the roadway—a powerful omen indeed. Fearful of recapture and overcome with the joy of his newfound liberty, Obama had not lingered in the avenue nearest his suburban Chateau d'If to masticate his tasty morsel but had rather slowed his pace for mere steps to scoop the furball in his jaws before continuing his flight, the fluffy tail lofting from one side of his clenched canines as he bounded across the asphalt and down the McMahon's drive into a backyard full of birdbaths and feeders hanging from every low-lying cedar branch, and all around him ubiquitous chirping and cracked sunflower shells piled up in deep mounds half-mingled with birdshit, from which sprouted the saplings of sunflower plants, where, here and there, some careless bird glutting itself fat at the feeder had dropped an unchewed seed into the fertile mixture of decaying mush below.

Carefully, sniffing and prowling low to the earth as he moved, Obama breeched the divide of the McMahon's shrubbery and belly-crawled his way onto the Cohen's patio, pausing first to ascertain the whereabouts of Kelley, the jowly pitbull-mastiff mix who owned the Cohen family and protected her clutch with enduring vigilance by seizing every possible opportunity to bark, bite, and otherwise intimidate any canine interlopers that dared impinge upon her sovereign lands. Upon recognizing Kelley's containment behind the plate-glass doors at the rear of the Cohen household, Obama dared to cross the scent-line of piss that demarcated Kelley's dominion from the remainder of the worldly realm. Watchful Kelley immediately sounded her most urgent alarm, but Obama saw no sign of human reinforcements in response to Kelley's call, and, while he moved to cross the Cohen territory posthaste so as to avoid calling undue attention to himself, Obama felt so jubilant in his freedom in the face of Kelley's restraint behind window glass that he allowed himself a brief pause in which to articulate his vainglorious correspondence onto the leg of a plastic chaise lounge beside the Cohen's covered-over swimming pool. He overran the Cohen's lawn, overtook the rampart of their raised-bed of alliums, and emerged again into the street, chomping victoriously at the prized furry lunch still in his jaws, and then, pausing momentarily, he downed his feast—bones, hide, and all—in a few assertive gulps.

Across the road lay The Great Expanse of mowed

grass, where the earth was clotted thick with the shameful reek of human scent, and where frequently there lingered specimens of the most grotesque human variety, cackling and cavorting about with their abominable offspring, wrinkled and writhing and disgusting in their hairlessness.

The Expanse was a source of no small trepidation for Obama, as it was the sight of a previous foiled liberation attempt. Months ago, during his Second Bloodless Liberation, Obama had misunderestimated the degrees of invisibility and anonymity afforded by "hiding in plain sight" and had been illegitimately incarcerated by unidentified human forces, whose motive for violent intervention into Obama's escape plans was unknown and could only be considered an unprompted act of war, given Obama's utter lack of a prior relationship—diplomatic, militaristic or otherwise—with said human parties. Had his fugitive status been betrayed by the clinking of the escape-signal chimes attached to the manacle about his neck? Or was it his choice of route? Perhaps he loped too close to one of the youngsters; it was best never to come between such feral beasts and their offspring.

Regardless, as Obama again found himself on the threshold of the terrible expanse, he resolved that this time would be different. He had been preparing for this moment for weeks—not only through the slow days of grueling tunneling through the earth, paw by paw, by which he had erected his covert aperture of escape, but also through a relentless commitment to scraping his neck-manacle upon the picket fence's bottom slats, which hung like stalactites from the roof of said escape tunnel, such that Obama had stretched and frayed his restraining device to the point where it still affected the appearance of integrity but could, when the time came, be, with some concerted effort, shed from over his ears. Thus naked and unrestrained he found himself prepared to retry his dangerous traverse. While crossing The Expanse remained a calculated risk, the prize of doing so justified the undertaking; on the opposite side of the field there yawned the mouth of an alleyway, wherein lay a treasure-trove to rival the Arthurian Grail or Ponce de León's Floridian Fountain of Youth: the scrap-filled dumpster of the local 24-Hour Chicken Hut Marathon franchise. A rusted-out portal in the corner of the dumpster allowed an intrepid adventurer to enter, summit the mountains of refuse, exorcise the territory of its entrenched raccoon population, and quarry for food to his heart's content. No worries there. Obama attained the alleyway and conquered the dumpster with the ease of a true conquistador.

Thusly, Obama had lived as chicken-fed royalty for the empyrean expanse of nigh on a week, gorging himself each night on still-warm buckets of country biscuits and artificially-seasoned thigh meat and spending his days either lazing in the shade of the dumpster on a bed of packing foam or roaming the hinterlands of the known world to scout the odorous fiefdoms of other lupine landlords in the attempt to ascertain whether he might recruit new allies to his crusade to transcend the brutal hegemonies of leash and muzzle.

On the seventh night, Obama returned home to find his pantry still unstocked for the evening. Whence his dinner? Whence his man-slaves? The alley was quiet. The raccoons had not attempted to retake the disputed theatre of the alleyway, and the restaurant itself was absent of its usual bustle of human voices and of the perfume of meatsmoke. Perhaps Obama had simply returned from his day's explorations before his regular feeding hour. No, something greater was happening. Obama smelled it on the wind, felt a trepidation in the air.

He waited. No food came.

Obama chewed a bur from his foreleg, licked and sniffed his other bodily parts in the necessary manners, and took a nap. He awoke. Still no food. Had Obama been able to read, he would've known that the Health Department postings in the windows of the restaurant not only explained the discontinuation of food service, but also offered warnings that should've averted him from consuming any remaining salmonellic food scraps. Had he foreseen the possibility of such scarcity, Obama might have rationed his earlier spoils. True, he had reserved a gnawed-clean stash of bones in the niche of a nearby oak's roots. But the satisfaction that these bones gave to him was something akin to what a human would experience upon gnawing at a stick of spearmint gum in lieu of a porterhouse and hollandaise-drenched asparagus tips.

Worse still, the retaining pond at the edge of the Expanse had dried up. Obama's tongue swelled and stuck to his palate.

The duty of demarcating his territory was made difficult by his inadequate reserves of urine; he could spare a mere drop at each checkpoint as he made his rounds from the fire hydrant at the alley's mouth to the yew tree in the lawn across the street to the mangled shopping cart twisted around the telephone pole, to the weeds at the edge of the loud place where the frightening things moved by at terrifying speeds.

Obama returned from patrol for his evening nap and slept straight through suppertime. No humans arrived to serve him. As evening wore on into night, he was too hungry to sleep and passed the time growling at the shadows of squirrels backlit by the setting sun. In his desperation, he began to reconsider his prior living arrangement with a sense of nostalgia he'd never thought possible. Whatever the drawbacks—limited opportunity for exercise, invariant menu, lowered self-esteem resultant from living on the dole rather than by one's own wits—it was clear that there were also attendant upsides to suckling from the teat of human servitude. He realized for the first time that in arranging for his freedom he had also abandoned his reign over his former realm, his role as master and protector, and the tributes (i.e. in the form of kibble) that his loyal subjects were required to tithe to him on a twice-daily basis. He had both escaped from prison and absconded from his throne. His belly groaned.

Obama fasted for two more days before he resorted to the dumpster's single remnant chicken neck, a disgusting tube of flesh gone black and maggoty, which he ingested and sicked-up, and when he made a recapitulatory second attempt to reclaim these nutrients for his bodily needs, he discovered again that the substandard foodstuffs refused to be contained. A feverish illness overtook him, and for two days he slept and only occasionally shuddered awake with fever-dreams that faded in the sunlight.

In his third day of attempted convalescence, Obama's fever worsened. His body was so racked by fatigue and dehydration that he passed the day in near total lethargy and rose only twice to mark his turf and to lap some pitiful tonguefuls of water from a fetid pool beneath a dripping air-conditioner at the rear of the alleyway.

If only he could have returned to Fort DeVries! He knew well enough the way home. Yes, "home" was indeed the right word for that place, prison though it had once seemed. He had been deluded to think otherwise. But he feared he could no longer survive the journey, no longer had the strength to carry his weary body from this end of the Expanse to the other. Sick as he was, he could only lay still and hope to recover.

So this was how he found himself—alone, sick, stranded—as the storm came on. Something dire brewed overhead. The sky was preparing for a great upheaval, swollen and sickly as Obama's belly. Thunder cracked. Obama mustered the strength to dumpster dive one last time and pulled free a greasy tarpaulin and a busted milk crate. He fortified his position by erecting the milk crate beside his cardboard mat and dragging the tarpaulin across, such that it folded on itself to form a bed and roof wall at once. It wasn't much, but it was something. A little shelter in the face of the coming storm. A little privacy in which to lie down to die.

# 4

# MINDY SEERSUCKER

So here was this old biddy trying to die on her, half her face frozen and her body shaking so bad the wheelchair might topple if Mindy didn't hold steady, her biddy body stinking of urine and weirdly of formaldehyde, or maybe not formaldehyde exactly but something probably carcinogenic. Or maybe that was just the taxidermied dog in her lap—Ladybird, a dappled dachshund six years gone that the old biddy still petted and spoke to as if she were alive. At least that's what she had done, Moira Doyle, the old biddy, before this stroke or whatever it was. Mindy cushioned the biddy's head as her seizure crescendoed, then gradually ceased.

She dialed Billie on her cell. Billie was supposed to be on call, and Mindy needed to talk to an authority figure so bad it wasn't even funny. She was alone—literally the only staff member at work this morning at Mother of Mercy Hospice—and here was this biddy trying to die on Mindy's watch and Mindy wasn't even a nurse, just an intern taking LPN night classes in her free time and she couldn't flippin' open the flippin' medical chart software to see flippin' what

37

this patient's flippin' prescriptions were and plus it might be the flippin' Rapture and Mindy knows deeply and truly Jesus Christ as her personal lord and savior, so if this is the flippin' Rapture what's she flippin' still doing here?

"God, forgive me for being a coward and a doubter," Mindy said. "I know You have a plan for me, Lord. I wouldn't be here if You didn't will it. So it must be a test, right? Of my faith? Because Jesus Christ is my savior and if this was the for-real Rapture I'd be gone, wouldn't I? Lord? It must just be a bad thunderstorm and maybe the nurses all got sick, maybe a flu is catching and I'm the only one who showed up for work today. Right, Lord? Lord?"

Mindy crossed herself. She dialed Billie again, shouldered her phone, and lowered the fence along the bedside. She set aside the taxidermal dachshund, scooped the biddy by the armpits, and dragged her atop the bed. The phone line pulsed. Mindy smoothed the scraggly hedge of hair from the biddy's forehead, which was blotched with sweat and caked face powder.

"Everything will be alright, Moira," Mindy said. She removed her rosary beads from her neck and coiled them around Moira's non-responsive hand.

"Do you want your Ladybird? Yes, you always do. There you go, there's Ladybird." The dachshund rested in Moira's lap, forever standing with a happy smile on its petrified face, as if waiting for a younger Moira to throw a tennis ball or Frisbee. Supposedly Ladybird had been a Best of Breed prizewinner in all the top competitions, back when she and her owner were both in better showing shape. Supposedly there was a boatload of trophies somewhere. In Moira's room, though, nothing. The dog collected dust in just the same way the trophies probably did, wherever they were. The room did contain a computer terminal, however, which displayed a login screen undershadowed by bold red words: *Due to too many failed login attempts, this account has been disabled. Please contact your network administrator.* Only there was no network flippin' administrator to flippin' contact, no other nurses, no anyone. Save God by her side, Mindy was alone.

She tried to remember what she'd learned in her nursing seminars. If this biddy was having a stroke that was one thing entirely—Mindy should be giving her the clot-buster drugs right away, the Activate or Atavist or Atavan or whatever it was called. But if the biddy was having a medication-withdrawal seizure that was another thing entirely, and Mindy didn't know if she should give her a dose of whatever drug she was withdrawing from to therefore end the withdrawal or if she should give her some kind of other drug entirely to cancel the symptoms, which was moot because she couldn't check the patient's chart to see the last time she'd had her diazepam and Percocet, if that's even what she was still on—Mindy thought that was correct but honestly didn't remember. There were no prescription bottles or paper records anywhere in the room, nothing in the cupboard but a flippin' dropper bottle of Patanol, which, the biddy didn't even have flippin'—Lord, forgive me—pink eye so why was that there?

"I'll be right back, Moira. I don't want to leave you, but I have to try something." Mindy rushed down to the pharmacy. The pharmacist had vanished, and the window to the cash register and storeroom was locked with a roll-down metal shade. Mindy stood alone in the darkened hallway with the dead fluorescents above her and way down at the end of the hall a single flickering bulb in a single far-off lamp. A minute passed. Another. Then Mindy hurled a waiting room chair against the metal curtain. The chair made the curtain bang like a snare drum but didn't bust it open, didn't even dent it so much as scuff its anodized surface.

As Mindy returned to Moira's room, she found herself hesitating outside the door. She was afraid of what she'd see inside, afraid and exhausted from looking after Moira and the other residents by herself, as she had been doing since early that morning when she arrived to find Mother of Mercy unlocked and unstaffed. She'd nonetheless begun making the usual rounds, although maybe fifty percent of the residents had disappeared from their rooms. At first Mindy stuck to practical tasks. If she stuck to practical tasks, she'd spend less time overthinking what was probably nothing, what was probably just a cold front and a bad bout of flu. She changed Bob's diaper. She log-rolled Terry, a blob of somehow-still-technically-alive human flesh, onto the side that currently had fewer bedsores. To Barbara she spoon-fed applesauce and Harriet she helped to dress. Harriet, with her wrinkled, desiccated old-person boobs all puddled up in her bra and her wrinkled, fat-rolled old-person stomach curled below it, who only ever wanted to wear the sweater she'd immediately taken off. Other nurses might insist that Harriet select another outfit so they could take the sweater to be washed, but the pathetic game of one-player-hide-and-seek that resulted was unbearable for Mindy, who, today, had dressed and re-dressed Harriet in the same sweater a half dozen times, and each time Harriet had more or less cried in joy. We want what we want, Mindy understood.

Take for instance, Walt. Walt wanted to yell, and as Mindy walked to and from the pharmacy, Walt had been yelling, "Baby, we should have gone to Vegas! We should've gotten hitched! Those bastards! Vegas! Bastards! I told you! Baby, we should have gone when we had the chance."

Mindy had also encountered a resident named Judith who'd escaped her room and taken a seat behind the front reception desk, picking up the phone and displaying puzzled reactions each time there was nobody on the line. Mindy knew how Judith felt. She'd felt this same sense of befuddlement moments before, when she'd attempted to go to the kitchen for some juice and had found that the kitchen no longer existed. It's not that the kitchen had been ruined or emptied or relocated; rather, through the kitchen door, the room itself just sort of wasn't. There was a white glow. Hazy outlines lingered in the air like the ghost of a kitchen, and Mindy's gut quivered with a repellant sensation, as if she had swallowed a massive magnet of the wrong polarity and the invisible fields of the kitchen were pushing her ever away.

Now, in the hall outside Moira's room, she collapsed into a waiting chair beside a potted ficus tree. Even if this biddy survived her stroke or seizure or whatever, she was likely to need meds that Mindy wouldn't know what they were or where to get them or how to dose them or whatever, and even if that didn't kill her, the no meds or potentially-wrong meds, she would need to be fed, and if she didn't starve, she'd probably flippin', who knows, drool herself to death.

Billie was still not answering her phone. Mindy tried her boyfriend Vonze. He wouldn't be of medical help, but if she got in touch at least maybe she wouldn't be alone. His voicemail said, "It's The Vonze. You know what to do."

"Vonze you gotta pick up, I need you so bad. What it is is that I'm at work and I'm all alone and there are all these old people and this one right here is flippin' dying, I think, in this room right beside me. Jesus Christ, forgive me. I'm scared, Vonze. Call me if you get this or come get me or come be with me. Or maybe if today is what it might be maybe you're gone already, which, I hope so, even if part of me hopes not. If you're still here, Vonze, say your prayers, please. God, please let Vonze be okay. I love you." Mindy tried Vonze several more times in a row. She called Vonze, and she called Vonze, and she called Vonze, and she called Vonze. She tried her mother, her girlfriends from youth group, Pastor John, her father away in Toronto. She tried 911 but the line was dead. Despite the accumulating evidence to the contrary, Mindy needed desperately to believe that she was not left behind. Maybe it was temporary. Maybe she just had some things to finish up on Earth before she went. Maybe God had called her here to help these people. Mysterious ways, all that. Perhaps an overtime, extra-credit type scenario? Yet here she was saying, yikes, God forgive her, basically the flippin' f-word in her thoughts over and over?

Alongside the ficus she knelt to pray but was immediately interrupted when something bumped her knee. Mindy opened her eyes to discover Ladybird beside her. Inanimate as Ladybird was, the dachshund had nonetheless come on a Lassie-like rescue mission to alert Mindy that Moira was in trouble, having been flung from the old biddy's lap by the onset of another seizure to bounce out through the door and into the hall, snapping Mindy from her reverie. Mindy scooped up the stuffed dog to return it to Moira's lap.

At the bedside, Mindy held the old woman's face in her hands. All these tiny blood vessels along the undersides of her nostrils had burst. The hair on her upper lip was crusted with dandruffy white flecks of dried spit. "It'll be okay, Moira. We'll figure it out, you old biddy, you lovely old granny, you child of God's creation. We'll get through this." Mindy squeezed the woman's hand. "Moira?" Was there something in return, a squeeze back? No, only a coincidence, another tremor of the old woman's ailing body. Her pupils rolled back, her eyes all whites. The seizure was worsening, a froth rising from her lips. A horrific strangled groan emerged from her throat.

"Please, God, please don't make me watch her die." Mindy couldn't bear to look at Moira, so she went to the window. The frogs had stopped raining but lay dead in the lawn, dead on the sidewalks, dead in caved-in craters of broken glass in the windshields of cars in the Mother of Mercy parking lot. The sky was still too terrifying to look at directly, and from the shiver that went through her spine and her very soul, Mindy knew it was an Act of God.

"Don't let this be the End of Days, Lord. This is a test right? Of my faith? It can't be the Rapture because I love you with all my heart, Lord. So why am I still here? I know I'm a sinner, and that's why Jesus had to die for me. I'm sorry for that time I almost smoked pot in Sarah Handi's car, and for being sexual with Vonze, and for how I halfway lost my virginity to him, and then later got angry at him for what Sarah said she heard from Laura about Vonze and that girl he works with even though that was all just gossip and lies Vonze said, and also for fighting with my mom, and for the times I denied you when I was with friends or at school and I was too weak-willed or felt somehow embarrassed, and for all the small lies and the lust and small ways of cheating or questioning my faith. Please forgive me. Don't let this be it. I'll do anything, Lord. Just don't let this be it, without me."

Before today, Mindy had always believed that in the face of adversity, she'd be a hero. Studious and athletic, standing atop the shoulders of $n^{th}$-wave feminism yet simultaneously clad in the armor of her faith, she could easily envision herself dashing into a burning orphanage to snatch endangered kiddos from the jaws of fate, plus shattering glass ceilings in her future practice as a biomedical engineer MD/PhD. But in the face of this particular adversity, Mindy was flabbergasted. There was no burning orphanage to rush into; she'd known no heroics. The challenge that came was the one she least expected: a challenge to her faith itself. She wasn't supposed to be left behind. She was supposed to be saved. She was saved, in her heart. She knew she was. So what the hell?

Mindy fell to the floor, and cried and prayed and cried until she could no longer cry, and then she managed to make it to her knees, to a proper penitent position. She prayed from all the chambers of her heart, pleading for forgiveness, professing her love, begging to be saved. Her final prayer was this: "God, give me a sign that you haven't abandoned me. Anything, God, to show me that you're with me, a phone call or a friend or a message or even a burning bush or a voice in my head or some miracle, whatever you see fit, just please show me something, please, please, please let me know I'm not alone."

Mindy waited. Nothing changed. Nothing arrived. No voice spoke to her. No inspiration welled in her. She climbed into bed beside the old woman, clutching her weathered hand as tightly as she dared. She snuggled up and supplicated herself beside the dying woman. She lay there with her sinuses burning with the ammonia scent of the woman's old piss and the weird carcinogenic smell of her dying body and the taxidermal dog atop her dying body, and the frogs' ribbits warbling in through the cinderblock walls, and the wind beating the windows, rattling the glass panes in their frames and whistling like breath through a tuneless flute, and the far-off medical beep of an EKG machine, and the constant whirr of a furnace or dehumidifier or other atmospheric appliance, and somewhere in the distance sirens sounding, and the shush of tires on pavement and the splash of tires through puddles, and down the hall an old man yelling against the void about Vegas and his lost love, and somewhere someone was weeping, and the clang of the metal grommets on the American flag outside the window snapping against the flagpole in the breeze, and the disquieting juxtaposition of a chickadee's birdsong in the midst of all of this everything else, and close by, the glottal groans of the not-yet-dead old woman on the bed beside her, the swish of fabric against the woman's twitching fingers, and closer still, the swish of her own hair across her ears and the nearly-inaudible shudder of her own shaky breathing and the utterly inaudible susurration of blood through an artery just below the delicate skin of her temple.

Still, she listened, waiting to hear His voice.

# 5

# PHILLIP "VONZE" DEVRIES

A frog had fallen into the uncovered Weber grill and flailed there on the grate with one leg broken and twisted between the wires. Another frog settled into the metal bucket of sand and cigarette butts below. Vonze stood as if watching inside the sliding doors that overlooked the smoking patio on their half of the duplex, but his attention was less on the gore outside than on his own reflection in the glass. He had a seventy-pound kettlebell in one hand, with which he was doing overhead push presses. Proper form was you stood in a wide, ursine sort of semi-squat, with your weight in your heels, maintaining a natural curve in your spine, and you breathed in and did a little preparatory bounce, and then, tightening your core and straightening your legs to lift out of the semi-squat, you exhale and propel the kettlebell overhead, mostly with your shoulders and triceps, but really your whole body is involved if you do the form right, which, that's why you keep an eye on your reflection in the window. Of course, with it raining frogs and everything, it was tempting for Vonze to look *through* his reflection, but at the same time Vonze knew it wasn't like the world was

47

ending or anything, and he had a half-finished shoulder routine scheduled for today that he wasn't going to let a storm get in the way of, no matter how many frogs fell from the stratosphere. He'd do a rep with the kettlebell, watch his reflection, release, look out the window at the frog-chocked lawn and the gloaming sky. Kettlebell, reflection. Release, window. Kettlebell, reflection. Release, window.

Vonze's grandfather Lewis, that old sonofabitch, sat in a nearby recliner watching television and lighting a cigarette. Lew had removed his respirator tube from his nostrils and tossed it to the carpet beside his oxygen tank in a perfunctory effort to keep the extremely flammable gas away from the extremely open flame. Vonze dropped his kettlebell on the protective rubber mat, crept up behind the recliner, and sneakily wheeled the oxygen away to a marginally safer distance at the opposite corner of the room.

"You know you can't do that, Pappy."

"It's not so dangerous as they say."

"You shouldn't even be in the same room with it. I'd be happy to help. I can carry you outside to smoke." Vonze returned to the kettlebell for his left arm reps.

"I'm not a helpless baby."

"I didn't say you were. I just don't want you to explode."

"Meh," Lew said.

It literally never occurred to Vonze that in such a scenario he, Vonze, too, might explode. As a categorical life philosophy, Vonze didn't believe that anything could kill him. He looked too good in a speedo. People who look that good in a speedo don't die. Dying was for pussies. Which Vonze was most decidedly not.[1]

"I dropped the damn remote under the COCKSUCKER. COCK. SUCKBUTTER COCKBUTTER." Lew's liverspotted hands went white and he clawed the arms of his chair. "Sucker. Suckbutter." As the fit passed, Lew crossed himself seven times, saying "Amen" with each gesture.

"Are you seeing what's happening outside?" Vonze said. "Looks like the end of the world out there."

Lew did not look. Lew had not looked away from the TV for literal hours. "Just a storm."

"Just a storm? It's raining frogs!"

"It'll blow over. Will you please get me the remote?" The old sonofabitch could hardly walk and was always asking Vonze to bring him his daily lunch of two Ensures and two Budweisers, or to run out to the Gas Rite for more smokes, or change his yellowed t-shirt, or etcetera. Vonze dug the remote from where it had fallen below the sofa. Lew surfed for a while, but nearly every channel showed static. Lew had this way of watching television that Vonze almost admired,

---

1 Yet here was his grandfather, sitting there dying right before his eyes, dying as hard as he could and smoking the shit out of cigarette after cigarette, just chasing death, just waving it in Vonze's face, just dying his hardest and doing his damnedest to show Vonze how wrong he was about everything. Or, rather, how utterly right he was in that tiny buried sliver of brainspace that was so very, very afraid.

that was really pretty next-level if you thought about it, the dedication it took to watch like that. Lew watched TV like Vonze hit the weights. He would slump in his recliner and not move for hours at a time, with a zen-like focus on the flickering images. But with the static, that wasn't possible. "First the COCKSUCKER cable goes, and now network."

"The antenna probably got hit by a frog."

"All yesterday I was thinking how at least we still got network."

"Seriously, it's raining frogs out here," Vonze said, and then, huffing under his breath, "Ten. Eleven. Twelve."

"'Cats and dogs' is the expression."

"Yeah, that's for when it's raining hard. This is for when it's raining frogs."

"What in God's name are you trying to say, boy? You make no damn sense. Always Twitter this and internet that." Lew had still not looked away from the television.

"I'm saying the thumping on the roof is not a hailstorm, Pappy."

The phone rang, and Lew smothered his cigarette butt in the ashtray.

"I'll get it," Vonze said, but Lew snatched the phone and shooed Vonze away. Vonze returned to his squat stance and held the kettlebell in both hands, the mass dangling like a heavy metal testicle between his wide-spread thighs.

"Hello? Who's there, MOTHERSUCKER. Sorry, I apologize. I have a condition. Please, who are you trying to—Obama? OBAMA COCKSUCKER MOTHER.

BUTTER. COCKBOTTOM COCK BUTTER. ROCK BOTTOM OBAMA COCK. Sorry, I can't control my—Hello? Hello?"

"Who was that?" Vonze maintained a backward thrust to his buttocks as he deepened the squat, all the while monitoring his reflection for a natural curve in the lower back. Even in the window's washed-out half-reflection Vonze could discern individual cords of muscle in his quadriceps, and this pleased him greatly. His triceps were looking pretty jacked, too. Plus his neck triangle things. All in all, he was pretty swole, if he said so himself.

Vonze had this whole system for training on a four-part cycle: upper body, lower body, cardio bursts, core/whole-body. Repeat. For upper body he did a crapload of towel flys and decline presses to really bring out the cuts in his pecs. It pretty much goes without saying that core days meant deadlifts, but he also did five or six hundred sit-ups daily, minimum, to keep the abs, which, that's what the cardio bursts were for, too, was fat cutting. He was twenty-two and he planned to look the way he looked forever. In last month's issue of *Men's Body* there had been a feature article on aging bodybuilders—guys in their 50s, 60s, 70s, all still looking jacked as all get-out. This one guy, they didn't even say his age, he was so old and you could see his face was hella wrinkled but he still had biceps like goose eggs and could probably crack walnuts by flexing his ass cheeks.

So that was the plan. To be that guy. To gain immortality through weightlifting.

Of course, living with Grandpappy Lew put some decided hurdles in front of the plan, since Lew was an enduring volcano of secondhand smoke and an effigy of bodily decay. He had one of those bladder jugs that trickled full of piss and had to be poured out manually into the toilet, which Vonze did several times a day. Vonze hated the old sonofabitch for subjecting him to this. Could there be anything worse in life than requiring a bag to piss in, and requiring a grandson to empty said bag of piss? Plus chronic pink eye, saggy man boobs and womanly jiggles of arm fat. Not to mention emphysema coughs so loud they woke Vonze every night, even though Vonze slept on an air mattress in the back bedroom and Lew slept upright in his recliner with the TV going. So it was pretty hard to forget the effects of mortality if you so much as set foot in the DeVries household. Still, Vonze did his best.

Not that it was even mortality that scared him. Not in the sense of being-aware-that-we're-all-going-to-die-type mortality concerns, anyway. Vonze had been a Marine. He'd seen death. Rather, it was decay that got him. The slow entropy of the body that could take a man like Lew—who had also been a strapping young enlisted Marine back in the day, and had snagged a real hottie of a wife (Yeah, yeah, so it's Vonze's grandma, so what? If you look at the pictures? Just saying.)—and transformed him into a puckered sack of meat with a slow-draining urostomy tube.

"Wrong number, I guess," Lew said. "They hung up. If it was someone who knew me, they wouldn't've hung up for a few measly 'cocksuckers.' Except the funny thing was they mentioned Obama."

"The president or the dog?"

"Dog, I think. But I don't want to get my hopes up."

"Maybe someone saw our posters?"

"I hope so. Or it could've been a political group. Except there was loud music in the background." Lew crossed himself seven times. "Amen. Amen. Amen. Amen. Amen. Amen. Amen."

"As long as it wasn't the guys from *Guts & Glory*."

*Guts & Glory* was Vonze's secret weapon, his plot to escape this Podunk town and make it to Hollywood to grab his fifteen minutes and then some; *G&G* was a reality television show to which Vonze had recently applied to be a contestant. He'd passed the first screening of a many-stage interview process and wanted nothing more than to get the next callback. *G&G* involved not only the familiar strongman competitions (e.g. dead lifts, caber toss, wearing harnesses and dragging airplanes down the tarmac, etc.) but also a series of increasingly stressful "bonus challenges," such as the "Fireman's Rescue," in which a dozen body-shaped sandbags were arrayed inside a burning building, and the contestant had two minutes to sprint around simulating a good deed for TV's sake by rescuing the would-be victims and hauling them outside to the "safe zone," or the "Stevedore" competition, in which the athletes stood on a dock and lifted heavier and heavier stones onto the nearby deck of a ship, with weights categorized in the traditional manner of Icelandic "lifting stones," namely, *fullsterkur, hálfsterkur, hálfdrættingur, and amlóði,*[2] or the "Kool-Aid Man" competition, in which competitors would hurl themselves, wrecking-ball-like, through a solid brick wall (sure, there was no mortar between the bricks, but, still, a brick freakin' wall).

The TV show's application process had involved producing a video resumé, for which Vonze had recruited various people in his life to act as impromptu camerapersons. Grandpappy Lew took footage of Vonze one-handing his most massive kettlebell like it weren't no thang. Mindy, his Christian girlfriend, went with him to Lake Kequanagaua for a stroll down the beach, capturing close-ups of his abs rippling and reaction shots of young MILFs ogling his glutes as he strutted past in his speedo. This section was meant to capture the "fun and quirky sides of [his] personality." (He was *fun*! He went to the *beach*! He wore an American flag speedo. *Quirky*!) The application had also asked him to submit some on-the-job shots, and he wished it would've been possible to splice in footage from his recent four-year stint in the U.S. Marine Corps, but he didn't have any footage, so Video Heaven it was. Vonze filmed a joke shot where he pretended to be weightlifting with concession stand candy that was way too heavy for him to lift. He hoped

---

2 Respectively: "full strength," 341 pounds; "half strength," 228.8 pounds; "weakling," 107.8 pounds; and "useless," 50.6 pounds.

that this would constitute "fun and quirky" as well. The workplace footage was shot by his co-worker Jeanine, who was the girl he was nailing because his Christian girlfriend Mindy wouldn't nail him until they got married, meaning she would never nail him. Actually, he wasn't nailing Jeanine, precisely, but they'd go for a spin in his pickup truck together most every lunch break and he'd drive with one hand on the wheel, the other alternating between the stick shift and the back of Jeanine's head as it bobbed up and down in his lap. On more than one occasion he had almost run a red light—it was sometimes hard to stay locked in on reality in the face of such distractions.

After Vonze did fifty reps of kettlebell swings, he moved on to a few dozen goblet squats. After a fifteen-minute break for his whey protein shake, creatine powder, and mid-morning hamburger, he restarted the workout circuit from the top with another set of overhead presses. In the middle of his presses, Vonze's cell phone rang. He sprinted to the kitchen. The *G&G* people would have a California area code, he thought, or maybe New York. But it was only Mindy. He let it go to voicemail—he wasn't about to abandon his routine halfway through—with the intent to call her back later. He was burly as hell, true, but he worried that he was only bare-minimum burly enough for *Guts & Glory*, so there was always more iron to be pumped. The phone rang again.

"Fifteen. Sixteen. Seventeen."

"You going to let that ring?" Lew called, "Or are you

going to answer the MOTHERSUCKER!"

"I'm in the middle of a set, Pappy. I'ma let the mothersucker ring."

"Don't you talk to me like that." Lew returned his lighter to its space in the cigarette pack and tossed the pack atop the coffee table. "You've got to take a break now anyway. I need my oxygen back."

"You talk to me like that all the time," Vonze said, abandoning his weights and retrieving the oxygen. Under his breath he said, "You old, old, old, sonofabitch."

"What was that?"

"Nothing, Pappy."

"Don't be a wiseacre." Lew again crossed himself seven times. In a moment of feeling "fun and quirky," Vonze joined him, and they performed this private liturgy together in chorus. "Amen. Amen. Amen. Amen. Amen. Amen. Amen."

Lew's channel-surfing had uncovered precisely two snowy channels transmitting some semblances of picture and sound: a woman hawking jewel-encrusted unicorn clocks on the shopping channel and *Jeopardy!*, which Lew hated. Vonze had heard him refer to the host, Alex Trebek, as a "pompous no-talent butt-wiping snob" on more than one occasion, but he now seemed to be watching *Jeopardy!* anyway. That is, until this picture, too, went out. Muttering, Lew uprighted himself and shuffled on his cane toward the sliding-glass doors.

"Where are you going, Pappy? Like I said, let me help."

Lew shooed Vonze off as if he were a nagging mosquito. "Keep doing your lifts, sonny. That's an order."

Vonze obeyed. Pappy Lew did, after all, outrank him. Plus it wasn't like he actually wanted to touch the old sonofabitch's greasy body if he could help it. He moved onto the split squats and counted off each rep with an "Amen." Squat. "Amen." Squat. "Amen."

"Jesus is Lord, that's a lot of frogs! The entire patio is covered! Did you know about this, boy? Why didn't you say something?" Lew swept the frogs from his path with his cane, prodding the living and flicking the dead, clearing a path to the patio furniture. He reached the nearest wire chair and stood resting both hands on its back. From the other side of the glass, Vonze watched Lew pick up a dead frog, dangling it by the foot so its bloated body swung from a rubbery leg. He brought the frog close to his face, squinting.

Vonze turned back to his reflection. Good thing he did, too, because his arm was supposed to be locked out straight with the kettlebell overhead for the split squat, and it was at a slight angle, so his back had rounded a little, which could have disastrous consequences. Nothing worse could happen to a lifter than a back injury. Vonze considered himself, oblivious to what was happening outside, where Lew stacked one patio chair atop another patio chair atop the wrought wire table, such that the whole contrivance climbed in the general direction of the TV antenna mounted at the corner of the roof. Lew shuffled atop the table, the metal groaning below him as the table legs flexed and its feet abraded against the pavement. The friction between the metal patio chairs caused them to murmur as Lew mounted first one, and then the second.

On the other side of the glass, Vonze was still contemplating his form in the mirror of the door, still guarding against that imagined back injury, because, see, if you twist an elbow or wrist? No big, you rest that side for a few weeks. Break a leg, you can still do bench press and battling ropes. But throw out a disc? You might as well start buying fat jeans and candy bars, because you were done for. Donezo. Done City. Get the hell out of Done.

Vonze rocked out fifteen more reps of split squats. On the sixteenth rep, a metal on metal screech broke his focus, and Vonze saw through his own reflection just in time to watch his Pappy fall.

# 6

## MINDY SEERSUCKER

The biddy was dead. Mindy had held her in her arms and watched the life go out of her. She sponged clean the body and crossed Moira's hands on her chest, clutching the rosary. Mindy said a prayer for Moira's departed soul and sat watching the corpse, half expecting it to levitate up to the heavens or simply fade away. When she was sure it would not, she left.

In the rec room, a couple residents napped in front of a TV playing static, leaning their heads together like two drunken airplane passengers on a redeye. Outside, a chicken-legged old man wearing only his boxer shorts was making a break for the bus stop. Normally, Mindy would've chased after and walked him back inside. But now? Let him go. Whatever bus the old dude got on—if he even got on a bus, if busses were even a thing that happened anymore— he'd probably end up better off than he'd be here trying to fend for himself. Mindy couldn't care for them all herself, and moreover, she couldn't save them all from whatever was happening. She couldn't save Moira, couldn't even save herself, apparently.

Exiting to the parking lot, she realized the rain of frogs had stopped. The frogs themselves seemed to be dissipating into drainage ditches and below bushes or wherever it might be that frogs went. The sky was bruised and bloodied. Not just bruised, but a whole atlas of contusions, a whole geography of dark and wrong and red expansiveness cut through by arcs of lightning. Did the air taste more like a progression or an aftermath? She wasn't sure. She'd asked Him for company and a sign, and God had given her death.

In her car, Mindy thumped her head against the steering wheel three times, then let it rest there, her bangs clinging damp between her skin and the vinyl. She dug a wad of Kleenex from the glovebox and used it to wipe away some of the splattered frogs and broken windshield glass from the dashboard. The car wouldn't start. The engine chugged then died. She waited a moment and tried again, to see if the car had maybe miraculously fixed itself. It had not.

She could call a tow truck, but what was the point? Nonetheless, she considered her phone anyway. She'd had a missed call while she'd been distracted with Moira's death. Vonze! He was still alive! Still on Earth!

She leapt from the car and began to run. His house was far, but not that far. She'd go to him, no matter what. If this was God's rapture or wrath, or a crazy terrorist attack or science experiment gone wrong, or the first winking glimpse of a nuclear holocaust—well, it didn't matter what it was. She'd be with him. But as she jogged past the other vehicles, she got another idea. No one was around to care if she borrowed one, right? She'd just have to find a car that had a spare key in a magnetic box under the bumper, or one that was unlocked entirely, as was not uncommon in safe, boring old Balta, Wisconsin.

The Volvo was locked. They were going to get married, her and Vonze. Sure, maybe Vonze hadn't asked her yet, maybe he didn't even know it yet, but she was pretty sure he knew it, based on the number of hints he had been dropping lately about the degree of, um, romance they were going to experience together. She knew he knew it. The rusty pickup truck was locked. So was the blue Toyota. He had to know it. She had told him so often of the southern-style farmhouse she wanted, with a long wrap-around porch on three sides of the building, on which to sit outside on summer days drinking lemonade and iced-tea and lawnmower beers, from which to watch her future children running through the lawn playing freeze-tag. She'd get her PhD and be empowered and all that, but she still wanted to be a wife. The sleek new sedan was not locked, but all she found in the glove box were maps and pens and a half-dozen condoms still in their bubble-packs. She wouldn't even mind if they got in mud-fights sometimes, the kids, and she had to put them in timeouts or take away their TV privileges. It was good for them, the kids, to spend some time in the real world and not in front of the TV, wasn't it? To be tangibly engaged in the sensory experience of the world? The next three cars were also unlocked, and she checked in the map slots and under the floor mats and in the glove boxes and there was nothing there at all. Wasn't it good for them to be getting their hands dirty and falling down and scraping their knees and hitting their thumbs with hammers while attempting to nail in boards for treeforts? Didn't that toughen them up mentally and strengthen their immune systems? She lucked out with the next car, a dun-colored jalopy of a VW Jetta. Mindy found a broken-off key in the ignition and a pair of needle-nose pliers conspicuously placed on the console, to be used to twist the key stump. So Mindy would let them run free, her future children, through the small copse of poplars and pines behind the house, and they could come and go as they pleased and dig through ancient metal coffee cans in the garage for rust-powdered nails to build their treefort together. She started the car and backed out of the spot, her hands sweaty and shaking and her guts quivering with excitement. She was on her way to find him. And they would build a home together, she and Vonze. Whatever this terrible new world was, they were in it together. The windshield was cracked and caked in blood, and she couldn't really see out of it, but she could kind of see out of it if she leaned sideways and down and looked through this one sort of clear spot. She would let them build the treefort together, the boy and the girl both, because they would be friends. She would teach them right, not to discriminate between the sexes, even though Julie, the girl, could still like dolls and the color pink for bows in her hair if she wanted to, but also use a hammer and drive dirt bikes, after she was old enough. Mindy wouldn't be militant. Mindy pressed the accelerator and veered toward the exit. She would head for Main Street via the Franklin Street Bridge and on to Vonze's house beyond. Julie, the girl, would still want to play tea time and have Mommy/Mindy show her how to bake pumpkin chocolate chip bread, and a bit of girly time was fine but it would be great, too, if she went outside with the boys and got dirty and nailed boards into trees and maybe even fell and broke her wrist, not that Mindy would ever wish that on anyone, especially not her own children, but sometimes what doesn't kill you only makes you—

A thud. Screaming metal. Mindy's head whiplashed and her seatbelt caught her, but not before she buckled two teeth on the steering wheel. Blood cascaded down her chin. Smoke billowed from the Jetta's crumpled hood. She had collided head-on with a big SUV turning into the parking lot just as she had been pulling out. She staggered out of the car. She turned, but didn't know where to turn. Somehow, she was outside herself. She was watching herself like a film. She was not here. She was sitting on her Southern wrap-around porch with Vonze and the babies, sipping lemonade in the summer shade. She was not here. She was not on the pavement beside a crashed and stolen car, was not holding her hands to her mouth to catch the blood, did not have two busted-out front teeth, had not come from a helpless morning of watching old people die, was not still on Earth when she should have been raptured, was not crying and spitting blood all over her pink sweater, was not trying and failing, was not feeling the liquid, thick and warm and wet as it slipped through her fingers, was not, was not, was not.

# 7

# Ralph Waldo "Obama" DeVries

Obama lay in his shantytown house in the alleyway behind the 24-Hour Chicken Hut Marathon deep in the throes of hallucination. The sky had become a whorl of meat and blood with yellow clouds like strata of fat in a marbled steak. Though he knew it was a vision and willed himself to snap out of it, he could not. For so long he'd yearned for rain and when the rain finally came his hunger-warped mind convinced him that it was Manna from heaven in the guise of amphibians. Not his first choice, but as they say, there's no condiment like hunger, and frog legs would do just fine, thank you very much, if only they were not hallucinatory. But Obama knew they were, for they had fallen in impossible amounts and filled the lawns, the sidewalks, the fountain in the parkway across the street, only that last part could never have happened because the fountain jiggled and flickered and disappeared.

But then a flubberly leg smacked him square across the nose—harder than any rolled-up newspaper—and everything changed. The recognition sunk in. It was real! Frog flesh all around him, and it was real! The Flood of

Glory was upon him. Obama ate until his belly ached, and then he ate more, and then he ate more. He was still too weak to walk, but he didn't have to—the frogs were so plentiful that he could simply snap at them from right where he lay, and his mouth would fill with frog flesh.

He was saved! He was triumphant! He knew well that his thirst was more dangerous than his hunger, and he lapped at a pool of splattered frog blood as it spread gradually closer. He ate and rested, ate, rested, ate. Aware that his convalescence was still nascent, Obama did not dare to venture too far but soon mustered the strength to visit the puddle below the drippy air conditioner for more hydration. This effort exhausted him, and afterward he lay again, half dozing, but startling awake whenever a terrible thunderclap rang out or he suffered a pang of indigestion as his belly burned through a too-big meal on a too-empty stomach. The sky boomed like a cannon, and Obama tunneled himself deeper under his tarpaulin, which foiled his attempts by snagging over his face and covering his eyes. Blinded, but only momentarily. He shook it off.

How pathetic he was, to cower here alone in the alley amongst human refuse and filth! How naïve he had been. What delusions of grandeur! He resolved to return to the DeVries estate as soon as he had recovered the strength to retrace his steps over the grassy Expanse. He would steer clear of any agents—human, canine, or otherwise—and return by the route he had taken, same hedge-holes and fence-holes, same avenues, maybe re-piss on the leg of that chaise if the bitch Kelley was still inside. He could see home already. He could smell the ambient cigarettes and taste the daily kibble. He could smell the human reek of the two manservants he kept in the house, both having the same familial stink of being each other's kin, but one sort of rancid with piss and decay, and the other constantly salty with his own sweat. Obama could feel the touch of the old one, scratching the undersides of his ears, hear his raspy, comforting voice. He was as good as home. He had only to rest and recover his strength and then the journey homeward would begin.

A horrible thought occurred to him. What if the DeVries had been unable to cope with their lives over these last few weeks without his leadership? What if they'd committed some grief-filled seppuku? What if, in their confusion and lack of direction, they had pledged fealty to another protector? What if they were, right this very moment, paying their kibble tithes to a canine mouth not his own? He had thought he'd wanted this escape from the duties of his kingdom, but he had been mistaken. Only when his former life was gone was he able to realize its merits. He had to get back, and quick. A new sense of purpose welled in him, and he rose to his feet. One step toward the mouth of the alley, and then another, hindquarters shaking with the effort. It was no use. His back legs crumpled below him. He rose again, teetered, and fell. Obama lay in the dampness of the frogblood-spattered alleyway. He hacked up a few spatters, but managed to avoid full-on emesis. Bodily cramps racked through him, and in the reverberating brick chasm of the alleyway, he whimpered a pathetic sort of whimper truly unfit for a ruler of his stature—a whimper of a sort that had not escaped him since he was a pup when he had nearly died once before.

He was seven or eight[1] at the time he first learned of his own mortality. Back then he was still hanging around with his litter-mates, who, like him, shared distinctive dappling, a tendency toward white boots, and either blue or brown eyes (he was the only sibling with one of each). They roamed free in those days, in the wilderness behind the ShopKo, which wasn't much of a wilderness at all, really—more like a sickly grove of sumac with decimated shopping bags windblown around the shrubby trunks and an abundance of crushed fast-food soda cups seeding the earth. Obama's mother had lived in the grove forever. His father had been a stranger-in-the-night type who had fled the scene long before Obama was born, one of a litter of five whelps who nursed side-by-side at their mother's hang-dog teats, wrestling in the open pavement of the parking lot, learning from their mother how to stalk a vehicle from a distance, to wait until its owners were gone, to sprint after their dropped hotdog or flyaway hamburger wrapper, which is what he was doing when he was hit by a rogue station wagon. It happened in slow motion, in the aisle of the ShopKo parking lot: the bumper connecting with Obama's

------

1 In dog years.

side, instantaneously snapping three ribs, flattening him to the pavement, concussing him and ripping the wind from his lungs. Obama gasped for breath and felt that mortal awareness settle over him like a long shadow.

Humans leapt from the car, squawking and squealing their nonsensical noises. From there, things changed quickly. He was denied a fair trial; in the corrupt human system, no official pronouncement of his guilt was necessary for them to toss him in the clink. For two straight days he wailed in lament of his false conviction, but no human nor canine was moved to his aide, and he finally resigned himself to his imprisonment and was silent. Hopeless, he could only lay in his tiny cell and nap. He lost track of time. Each day was like the next: despite his incarceration, he was given a servant who kept him fed and whisked away his stools. This servant was also a sadist, though, capable of inflicting bee-sting pain from shiny implements of unknown intent, and willing to host random visitors to Obama's chambers at all hours of the day, heedless of Obama's privacy and eager to interrupt regardless of whether Obama had been preoccupied in profound meditation or in giving himself a bath.

One of these sets of visitors were the DeVries, whose visit at least had a purpose; they were there to introduce themselves as his new wardens and to transfer him to a minimum security facility on account of his good behavior. Or so he'd thought at the time of his first imprisonment in their home, in which he was still restrained but was given comfortable furnishings to lie on, rawhide bones to chew, and no shortage of groomings, massages, and babytalk.

But now, in the alleyway of his despair, Obama began to understand his past differently. He had always associated the car accident with his capture, but he began to see that from a human point of view, it had been a rescue. They'd believed him to be hurt, as indeed he had been. He'd known true fear, glimpsed the darkness on the other side. Now, in his state of semi-starvation, seeing that darkness again encroaching, Obama could no longer doubt his captor's good intentions; they'd believed they were helping him.

Surely part of his desire for escape had stemmed from the wild freedom of his upbringing. His nostalgia was the common nostalgia anyone might have for childhood days of carefree playing and running, but that wasn't the whole story. In his selective memory, he had blocked out the downsides of freedom: the accident, the harsh realities of living in a median behind a mini-mall. This had been a time of scarcity, a time of chewing the tail off roadkilled possum and licking ketchup remnants from empty paper plates, a time of sleepless nights when the rain fell through the sumac leaves, a time of frightening noises: vehicles that emitted thunderous bursts of bass as they drove by, screeching human children, street sweepers whirring their metal baleen brushes along the curbs outside the copse. He was mistaken to remember only the golden moments of his youth, and to forget the shivering, the nigh-starvation. These revelations of memory only increased his newfound resolve to return home to the DeVries. Once again, he rose to shaky feet. Step by painful step he worked his way out of his hidey hole and toward the mouth of the alley.

But just as he did so, new adversaries appeared. Two silhouettes guarded the mouth of the alley. Humans. Elongated shadows with terrifying talons, clothed in the stinking hides of slaughtered animals. Even from here Obama could smell the reek of leather and resinous smoke layered with all other manner of organic volatiles.

Obama's hackles raised. He would not again let outsiders foil his plans, not now, when he had only just resolved to take action. If he could have communicated with them, he would have told the humans that there was no need for them to take him prisoner, he was going home anyway, and he didn't care whose partyline they adhered to in the brutal dichotomies of the canine/human slave trade. But these savages, like all humans, were stupid. They could only grunt and squeal; they had no sensible means of communication. Still, what choice did he have but to try? Mustering himself through the pain, Obama rose to his feet, growled, and bared his fangs.

**8**

# LYLE DENIAL

The last minor chords of *Lock Up the Wolves* faded from the interior of the bitchmobile. In the pseudo-silence that came after, the muffler-rattle and phlegm-hacking sputters of the vehicle's unfortunate mechanics sounded all the more pronounced, even as the wind howled and thunder cracked. Lyle's ear had grown accustomed to the croaking of the frogs, the hugeness of it, a sort of Phil Spector wall-of-sound style production. He should've brought his sampler; it would make a great found-sound backing track for an ambient record. The front of the pickup had become an unfortunate museum of frog anatomy. When he sprayed the washer fluid, the wipers only smeared things so the chunkier bits of gore were swept clean, but the twin red streaks that arced across the windshield like a double rainbow, well, those weren't going anywhere.

Trevor, using a stick of beef jerky as a pointer, indicated the 24-Hour Chicken Hut Marathon restaurant. "You want to get some lunch?"

"Hell no," Lyle said, but he pulled into the parking lot anyway, parked, and rolled his window down for a clear

71

view. "Besides, it looks like nobody's home. Probably nothing left but frozen chicken meat or maybe no freezers and the chicken's all raw and maggoty, and no way am I eating salmonella or, worse yet, working the fryers myself. Been there, done that, never again. Plus, are those Health Department warnings in the windows?"

"So why are we parked?"

"I thought I saw something in the alley back there. A dog." Lyle used his sneaker to scrape a frog-free landing zone before he stepped from the truck.

"So all the sudden it's We're-Rescuing-Every-Random-Dog-We-See Day?"

"So what if it is? I'm having a... what do you call it? Revolution? Realization? Like maybe this is my calling. Not just Ladybird and Obama, but *all* the dogs. Maybe I'll go door to door and fill up the whole pickup and adopt them all. Maybe we'll live together in a big dog mansion, if I can find a mansion that no one lives in and also isn't disappered."

"Why?"

"Because look around you. Because who'll help them if not us? Because seriously what are they going to do without their people?"

"I don't know, eat frogs."

"Yeah? How would *you* like to eat frogs?"

"I imagine that if I were a dog, brah, I should like very much to eat a frog."

The current dog in question lay beside a dumpster in the

alleyway behind the restaurant, nestled amongst the rubble with his butt backed into an impromptu cave of boxes and tarpaulin, like a dragon slumbering in the mouth of its gold-filled cavern—only a mangy, bloodshot, ribs-through-skin sort of dragon.

"This lil' dude needs help," Lyle insisted. "He looks sickly."

"He looks pissed, is what he looks. What if he has like rabies and like bites you and you like die of hydrophobia."

"He looks tired is all. Not rabid."

"Fear. Of. Water."

"C'mere boy. C'mere. What's your name, boy?"

The dog's teeth were bared, but at the same time it struggled to hold open its eyes.

"Give him a beef jerky."

"That's my lunch."

"Which I got for you, which we can get more of, since nobody works anywhere anymore. Here, boy! C'mere, boy!"

The mutt put his paws to the earth and stretched through alternate rounds of *Adho Mukha Svanasana* and *Ūrdhvamukhaśvānāsana*.[1] His legs quivered and his tail hung limp. Lyle reached out, but the dog would not close the gap between them.

"Holy shit, I think that's Obama."

---

1 Downward-facing dog pose and upward-facing dog pose, respectively.

"Get real. Just get the hell real, hombre."

"I'm real. Open my email and read me the part about Obama." Lyle's attention flicked momentarily skyward as a massive lightning bolt cleaved the mouth of the bloody gyre that continued to expand overhead.

"Okay okay okay okay. Um, okay: Ralph Waldo Obama DeVries, dog slash mutt, em, blah blah, white boots, one blue eye one brown, approx. forty five libs. Holy pope shit, I think you're right! Except he doesn't look forty five libs."

"He might if he were healthy. But he has the boots and the weird two eyes. Obama, c'mere boy! Here, Obama!"

The dog's ears perked at the sound. Hesitantly, it approached. Its neck was scrawny but its belly looked swollen and distended, like one of those sad little children in a pennies-a-day ad.

"Obama! That's a good boy. Here, Obama!"

Lyle extended some jerky as a peace offering and Obama sniffed it from afar and then all at once pounced, a cascade of slobber splattering down the arm of Lyle's black leather jacket.

"Gross," Trevor said.

When Lyle attempted to pet Obama, the dog flinched away, so instead Lyle stretched a hand back until Trevor got the clue and palmed him another piece of meat. He let Obama take his time with the treat, let him lick the salt from his fingers before he attempted to pet him again, but when he at last made contact, Obama seemed to welcome it and to push back against Lyle with his own body. Lyle drew the dog close, scooping it up in his arms. Obama nuzzled him. There was an eagerness in his eyes, those wet obsidian orbs that were somehow so much more expressive than they had any right to be. Lyle understood those eyes. He understood the muzzle nestled up in the crook of his neck, and he understood more than that, too—that like Lyle himself, the dog had been frightened, sick, and alone. That, all along, Obama had been right here, waiting for him.

# 9

# T. WODEHOUSE BRINKLEY

"Jesus, how'm I supposed to know what effect this'll have on interstate transit time, Gary?" Randy Brinkley said, driving. "Well, clearly negative. Clearly. But what I'm saying is it may be too soon to predict the full scope of the thing." Wode could hear his father's voice but could not see him, as he was sitting solo in the rear seat of the Land Rover wearing the Eyebeam goggles. At the moment, *Nether Realms* was on pause as Wode had just died ten times in a row and was taking a breather to mentally strategize his next attempt at slaying the Beholder.[1]

---

1 A car-sized orb of floating flesh with a single massive eye above its shark-fanged mouth and a dozen lesser eyes rising on lobster-like eyestalks, The Beholder was a potent magic user, as each eye was capable of casting a different spell. The central eye led the attack by emanating a wavering cone of anti-magic that canceled Wode's/Lothar's gnostic attacks and left him only melee options, which were proving pretty useless, given the casting abilities of the stalked sub-eyes, which included "Disintegrate Objects" (Level 7), "Transmute Flesh to Stone" (Level 3), "Cause Sleep" (Level 8), "Levitate" (n/a), and worst

76

He needed a plan. But with his soundtrack muted, Wode realized that the other background sound he'd been hearing was his mother crying. He removed his Eyebeam to see how she was doing, but he couldn't reach her from where he sat, plus a spontaneous flash of gaming insight just then overtook him.[2] Again he returned to his virtual world.

"I can assure you, Gary, that I am doing my damnedest to, as you say, quote 'unfuck the situation ASAP,' end quote, Gary, I can assure you that much."

Cell phone in hand, Wode's father drove single-handedly, palming the wheel. At occasional brief interims, he reached to adjust the radio or thermostat, or to squeeze his wife's shoulder where she sat crying into her hands in the passenger seat. This is how Randy came to be driving no-handedly when they hit the car—THUD—and came

---

of all "Charm Humans" (Unknown, probably level 10+, given that it worked on Wode/Lothar every time and rendered useless his "spell-catcher" passive ability, which, at level 12, was pretty well jacked).

2 Wode/Lothar would leave aside the Beholder's lair for a moment to go level up against some lesser monsters, and when he'd accumulated sufficient XP, he would upgrade his own anti-magic spell, so that he would anti-magic the Beholder before the Beholder could anti-magic him, thus reversing their roles—Lothar the Destroyer would retain the power of sorcery, while the Beholder would be robbed of its strongest attacks, and, sure, it's bite still stung, but really, what was a bite compared to getting hit with a Level 7 Disintegrate Object?

to a whiplash stop in the mouth of the Mother of Mercy parking lot.

Wode felt the impact and heard his parents yelling, but he was mid-melee with some nasty undead foes so he took a minute to finish up before he removed the Eyebeam. Randy had driven smack into this crap-colored little beater, and the girl who'd been driving had gotten out and was stumbling around in stupid circles on the pavement, like a confused bumblebee. Blood soaked the front of her shirt. She held a hand to her gushing mouth, blood seeping through her fingers.

"Oh God," Eileen said. "Randy, look what you've done!"

"What *I* did?" Randy said. "She was the one who hit me!"

Eileen leapt from the car and wrapped the girl in a hug. Although Wode couldn't hear their conversation from inside the car, he could see everything he needed to see in their body language. His mother was, well, mothering this girl. Wode hacked up a loogie, muddled it around on his tongue, and swallowed it back down, though he knew it would just come back up again if he didn't spit it out. Wode understood his complicity in his recent distance from his mother—his adolescent embarrassment at being seen with her, the beeline he made for his bedroom every afternoon when he got home from school, the hours upon hours spent immersed in the virtual world inside his Eyebeam helmet, to the point where his mother had given up yelling at him to take it off, and his father had given up trying to physically drag Wode from his bedroom to the dining table, and instead they just left a plate of food on the table, steaming and then growing cold, and then eventually they put the plate into the fridge under plastic wrap, which Wode would peel off sometime around midnight when his hunger pangs grew to interfere with his gaming performance. So, yes, Wode blamed himself. But that fact didn't negate the jealousy he felt at seeing his mother mothering someone else. Rather, his lingering sense of complicity made his self-hatred worse, which made him deny his self-hatred more strongly, which made him all the more angry at his mother. Wode stepped out of the car, on the opposite side of the vehicle, where he wouldn't have to look at them. He could still hear the girl crying and his mother soothing her.

"Are you alright?" Randy was saying. "What's your name?"

"By teef hut. Uzz eyes fnn. Mndy."

Curiosity got the best of Wode, and he peered around the hood of the car. The girl Mandy made bloodied eye contact with him. Eileen had her arms around the girl's shoulders. Randy stripped off his button-down, followed by his cotton undershirt, which he wadded up.

"Hold this to your mouth, Mandy."

"MNN-dy," the girl said.

"Why don't I stay here with Mandy, Eileen, and you can go inside and check on your mother?" No sooner had Randy spoken than Eileen was already disappearing toward the facility.

"MNN-dy," the girl said.

"Yeah," Randy said, "I know. Hold it up there, honey, it'll staunch the blood."

But Mandy was not staunching the blood, she was allowing the blood to flow freely from her mouth and down her chin and to drip onto her pink sweater as she gaped open-mouthed in the direction of the street. Wode followed her gaze and located the object of her attention: some dude was carrying another dude down the street, and not merely lifting him but actually running with an effortless strength, sprinting almost, huffing audibly even from this distance, but otherwise seeming totally unfazed or unaware even of the added burden of a whole 'nother human body in his arms. The younger man had the older man cradled up as if he were a bride or a newborn baby and was running right down the middle of the street, cutting between the abandoned cars that had created a roadblock in the middle of the throughway, headed right toward them. He looked like a superhero. He was just the sort of burly, ripped, jacked, swole, thewy, mesomorphic, heroic beefcake that Wode had so often wished he could magically transform himself into.

The older guy, the guy who was being carried, vaguely resembled the young guy via their matching buzzcuts, but he was also wrinkled and liver-spotted and generally softer. The old guy cradled something in his own arms: an oxygen tank, leading to a breathing mask, leading to his nostrils. His eyes were closed in a rictus of pain, and his whole lower body was twisted up in an impossible geometry—clearly, he had suffered some serious breakage in the hips or femurs or both or more.

"Vnnng! VNNNG!" Mandy squealed, hopping up and down, blood spraying from her mouth. "Vnnng!"

"Oh thank God I found you," the man apparently named Vnnng said, closing the distance between them.

"Yuh cm fuh muh!" Mandy said.

"Of course I did, babe," Vnnng said. "Plus, Pappy Lew had a fall and needs medical—" He shifted the old man's weight into a single arm and embraced her with the other, leaning as if to kiss her lips, but at the sight of her busted face he redirected to her cheek. "Uh—what happened to your face?"

Mindy gestured to the imploded SUV.

"A car accident?" Vnnng said. "Are you okay?"

From where he leaned against the SUV, Wode watched their embrace with a half-boner, wishing it were he who was being embraced. She was pretty easy on the eyes, Mandy was, even without front teeth and with blood all over her sweater.

Vnnng placed the old man gently in the grass. "We have a serious casualty here. Pappy Lew took a fall, and on the way here there was a traffic jam of abandoned cars blocking the whole bridge and I had do like a manual cas-evac and run him down here, as you can see."

Randy nodded to Vonze with the silent confidence of two grown men who knew that words weren't necessary—a gesture that Wode felt utterly incapable of; he was still a boy, hiding behind a car while the men did their manly things. Randy knelt over Lew to assess his condition. "He needs a doctor," Randy said, as if anyone doubted it.

"Are there doctors here? Is anyone left?" Vnnng said.

Mandy shook her head. "Jss me." Blood wept from her mouth, and she dabbed at it with the soiled undershirt.

"Please, allow me." Vnnng shredded Randy's bloodied undershirt into strips. "Open up," he told the girl, and he tied the cloth into her mouth like a gag, saying, "This way your hands will be free to help and do nurse stuff." She smiled through her bloody gag.

"That a girl," Vnnng said.

Her mouth bound, the girl knelt over the old man and got to work. Wode watched for a minute and then he didn't. Without even realizing it, he had donned his Eyebeam goggles. He wasn't gaming, but he breathed and listened to his breath in the comfort of his blocked vision, the world removed.

"Wode? Are you over there?" Randy called. "Look inside the car and see if there's anything we can use for a splint or a cast, like a stick or a blanket."

Wode attempted to turn invisible.

"Wode? Did you hear me?"

"Yeah, okay, Dad," Wode said, unveiling his eyes. But he was distracted by a sonic chaos descending on them. A pickup truck blaring heavy metal screamed around the corner of the hospice building, fishtailing and tires squealing. The pickup was encrusted in a maroon and green armor of congealed frog parts, and a half-dozen dogs were in the pickup bed, their ears blowing back, the tongues lolling joyfully in the wind, some howling along like coyotes in accompaniment to the screaming metal guitars. The truck whipped a few doughnuts in the empty lot and then came screeching to a halt not far from where they stood. For no reason whatsoever that Wode could discern, the ripped superhero dude started jumping and fist-pumping and yelling, "Obama! Obama!" at the top of his lungs. He ran over and lifted one of the dogs from the pickup bed, twirling around in circles with the dog in his arms like two lovers reunited in a meadow in a movie. Mandy watched with tears in her eyes. Even an emotional dunce like Wode could discern that she was jealous of the dog. Others of the pups leapt out and ran wild through the lot, while the remainders yipped and zipped in circles in the bed of the truck. The two guys who got out of the cab were dressed in badass black leather and spikes, one with long black hair and the other with a huge goatee and shaved head, both tattooed in places no sane people had tattoos, both quaffing beers in public in the middle of the day and chomping heartily on strips of beef jerky.

"Do you know this Obama?" one of the rockers was saying to Vnnng.

"Who are these fools?" Randy whispered to Wode. "I don't like their looks."

"They're just metalheads, Dad. Don't judge."

"Okay, buddy," Randy said unconvincingly. "Say, new idea. Why don't you go inside the hospice and see how your mother is doing with grandma. And grab some ice and some aspirin, or whatever you can find to help Lewis and Mandy here. I'll stay here and keep trying to help."

"Okay, I guess. But I don't know what to do, Dad."

"Neither do the rest of us, buddy. Just man up and do your best. "

Man up. Okay. Wode nodded. Reflexively, he pulled his Eyebeam goggles on, blocking his vision. For a few long breaths he kept his eyes closed. His hand found the power switch, but did not turn the game on. His fingertip lingered there, itching. He rocked the switch quickly on, and then off again before it could boot up. On, then off. He was tempted. So, so temped to not engage with reality. But, finally, Wode removed the Eyebeam helmet. Like, he actually removed it from his head. He actually went ahead and set it down on the ground, left it on the earth. Did not picked it back up. For the first time in who knows how long, the device was no longer in physical contact with his body. He yearned to return to it, but he walked away, headed toward the hospice building. But suddenly the hospice was not there. Wode broke into a run, but there was nowhere to run to. The building was gone.

"Mom?" Wode cried. "Mom!"

Where the building had been there now stood nothing but a hole, though "hole" was not even the right word for what was left. It was a weirdness, a whiteness, a void that you couldn't really look at, couldn't really see. You could try to look straight on, but it defied comprehension. It was less a physical thing, more an absence.

"Wode! Get away from there! What are you doing?" his father called.

"Hey little bro, I wouldn't," one of the metal dudes said.

Wode didn't listen. Something was defrosting. Something was sublimating. He felt as if he had been looking at the world in two dimensions for so long and had just realized that there were three, and suddenly he, well, he doesn't know what, exactly, but in this moment he all at once feels actualized somehow. Somehow, he no longer was or will be. Somehow he is.

Wode walks to the very threshold of this weird whatever-it-is. It is not a pit, nor a cavity, nor a crater, nor a space, nor a gulf, nor a chasm, nor a crevasse, nor a divide, nor a vacuity, and not even really a rift, though perhaps rift comes closest. It is a nothing and a something at the same time, a sort of blinking sensation and whiteness and glow that seems to have an edge and also seems imperceptible, a flicker, a jitter in the vision and a momentary void in sound, but Wode can somehow see through it and around it and all the rest of the world is still there, and all the rest of the world is inside the whiteness, inside and outside simultaneously, and the rift is both there and not there at once. It is not the emptiness of an unlived-in house, nor the whiteness of the virtual page when the words are deleted from the screen, nor the ambience of the atmosphere itself when no birds sing and no winds blow. It is not an absence nor an aperture nor a gap. It is simply a ______________. That's what it is.

Wode inches to the edge of the ____________, toeing forward until his sneaker tips have crossed its threshold and his toes have sort of curled over, though there's nothing really to curl over so much as to just sort of bask in this pulse and glow and feel this invisible membrane demarcating a divide, how a mosquito's feet must feel as it walks over the surface of a soap bubble. Wode tests the membrane a bit more forcefully with his toe, as if he might feel whether it is permeable or not. He thinks of the bug in the code of *Nether Realms* wherein one's avatar gets stuck both within the wall and without and wonders if this is what has happened to his mother, if she is stuck somewhere within something, whatever or wherever that something might be, or if she's gone: raptured, evolved. Wode's foot feels aglow, like his bones are radiating white light, and he presses a little harder, and knows that if he walks out into this ____________, its weight will hold him. He shifts his weight to stride, but hesitates for a last look before he steps onto the ____________. Wode turns back to face his father and the injured girl his father is hugging, the ripped dude cradling the dog, and the metalheads crowded close behind them, all walking toward him, all together, everyone together in this weird, hurt, collapsing world, and his father's hand is outstretched as if to clasp Wode's own, desiring to close the distance between them, and everything seems to have taken on a sort of gauze over it, so Wode is speaking but can't hear himself, he's reaching toward them in his mind but can't seem to reach with his body, wants to clasp his father's outstretched hand but can't quite get there, can't concentrate in the midst of all that glow and all that echo and whitewash and hum, yet he knows that he must reach him, that although the ___________ is taking him, there is nothing more important than now, this stretch, this moment—he mustn't wait any longer, he mustn't defer responsibility, he must act, must finally close the distance between them. And this, this is the only thing that matters.

# Acknowledgements

I am gratefully indebted to the crew at Etchings Press for believing in my work and for all the loving labor they put into bringing this book to life. Thank you to Jeffery Dixon, Mercadees Hempel, Spencer Martin, James Nelligan, and Kevin McKelvey. Many thanks to my early readers, whose feedback proved invaluable: Hannah Oberman-Breindel, Lydia Conklin, Yuko Sakata, Marian Palaia, Meghan O'Gieblyn, and Barrett Swanson. And to Kerry, for everything.

# About the Author

Christopher Mohar has been the recipient of a Wisconsin Institute for Creative Writing Fellowship and *The Southwest Review's* McGinnis Ritchie Award for fiction. His work can be found in *The Mississippi Review*, *North American Review*, *Creative Nonfiction*, *Arts & Letters*, *Gastronomica*, and elsewhere. He lives in Madison, Wisconsin, with his wife, daughter, and a chicken named Duck.

# Colophon

The main body, front matter, and back matter text is set in Baskerville with the narrator headings in Baskerville Bold. The front title, title page, and the chapter numbers are set in UnifrakturCook. The back cover material is set in Avenier.

# Etchings Press

Etchings Press is a student-run publisher at the University of Indianapolis. Each year, student editors choose the Whirling Prize, a post-publication award, in the fall and coordinate a publication contest for one poetry chapbook, one prose chapbook, and one novella in the spring. For more information, please visit etchings.uindy.edu.

Previous winners and publications

**Poetry**
2019: *As Lovers Always Do* by Marne Wilson
2018: *In the Herald of Improbable Misfortunes* by Robert Campbell
2017: *Uncle Harold's Maxwell House Haggadah* by Danny Caine
2016: *Some Animals* by Kelli Allen
2015: *Velocity of Slugs* by Joey Connelly
2014: *Action at a Distance* by Christopher Petruccelli

**Prose**
2019: *Dissenting Opinion from the Committee for the Beatitudes*
        by Marc J. Sheehan (fiction)
2018: *The Forsaken* by Chad V. Broughman (fiction)
2017: *Unravelings* by Sarah Cheshire (memoir)
2016: *Pathetic* by Shannon McLeod (essays)
2015: *Ologies* by Chelsea Biondolillo (essays)
2014: *Static: Stories* by Frederick Pelzer (fiction)

**Novella**
2019: *Savonne, Not Vonny* by Robin Lee Lovelace
2018: *Edge of the Known Bus Line* by James R. Gapinski
2017: *The Denialist's Almanac of American Plague and Pestilence*
        by Christopher Mohar
2016: *Followers* by Adam Fleming Petty